MOOCHING
MOOSE &
MUMBLING
MEN

Other Books By Joe Back

Horses, Hitches and Rocky Trails

by Joe Back

The Sucker's Teeth

by Joe Back

The Old Guide Remembers

and

the Young Guide Finds Out

by Joe Back, with Vic Lemmon

MOOCHING MOOSE & MUMBLING MEN

Stories and Illustrations by

JOE BACK

JB

JOHNSON BOOKS

AN IMPRINT OF BOWER HOUSE

DENVER

Mooching Moose & Mumbling Men: Stories and Illustrations by Joe Back. Copyright © 2020, 1987, 1959, by Joe Back. All rights reserved. No part of this book may be used or reproduced in any manner whatsoever without written permission except in the case of brief quotations embodied in critical articles and reviews. For information, contact Bower House: BowerHouseBooks.com.

Printed in the Canada
Designed by Margaret McCullough
Illustrations by Joe Back

Library of Congress Control Number: 2019957229
ISBN 978-1-55566-479-4

10 9 8 7 6 5 4 3 2 1

Author's Note:

This is all fiction. I hope it sounds real. I hope too that no one will try to identify defunct or living people or animals with the characters in this book. It just ain't so. Nosy is a piece of fiction too.

—J.B.

TO ALL TELLERS OF MOOSE TALES:

IF YOU CAN BEAR TO HEAR THE TRUTH YOU'VE SPOKEN
TWISTED BY A KNAVE TO MAKE A TRAP FOR READERS.

CONTENTS

CONTENTS

Introduction

Joe Back was born April 12, 1899, in Montpelier, Ohio. His father was a country doctor who visited his patients by horse and buggy. A lover of horses, he maintained a breeding stable when not practicing medicine. Through him, Joe developed knowledge of horses at the earliest age, handling the buggy as his father made his rounds.

When Joe was only 9 years old his father died of a sudden heart attack. His mother relocated to California where she soon remarried. Joe could not get along with his stepfather who was quite a drinker; so when he got in trouble at school for drawing sketches of his 8th grade teacher, he decided that was enough of that whole situation and took off on his own.

Joe's mother had a cousin who managed the Fiddleback Ranch north of Douglas, so Joe headed there and was put to work as a choreboy for board and room. Having learned to handle horses from his father, he was soon promoted to full ranch hand status with wages of $45 a month.

With the onset of World War I, Joe entered the Navy. Proficient with firearms, he was assigned to be a machine gun instructor and the closest thing to an ocean he ever saw was Lake Michigan. Discharged in 1919, Joe returned to Douglas and began cowboying on the 55 Ranch for ranch foreman Wheeler Eskew. Wheeler was a top hand and Joe considered him "one of the finest men I ever got to know."

Joe had filed on a homestead 42 miles north of Douglas and had begun the improvements necessary to obtain full ownership when he heard about a big horse roundup. Hiring on with 6 or 8 other cowboys, they eventually caught several hundred stray horses, which were to be purchased by the Diamond G Guest ranch above Dubois. They then obtained a chuck wagon and rope corral and herded the horses from Douglas to Brooks Lake and the Diamond G, a distance of approximately 270 miles. The trip took 2 weeks and was filled with adventure.

The Diamond G wanted Joe to stay on as a wrangler and guide, so he leased the grass on his homestead and remained in the mountains.

xi

He began guiding summer pack trips in the Teton Wilderness, including trips as far as Lewis Lake in Yellowstone National Park. In the fall, he would guide elk, deer, and bighorn sheep hunters.

Joe Back had always liked to draw and sketch and the Brooks Lake country was full of subject material. He began making sketches of horses, mountains, and cowboys and gave them away to ranch guests. One summer-long guest was Louis Agassiz Fuertes, a staff artist with National Geographic. When he saw Joe's sketches, he encouraged him to attend the Art Institute of Chicago.

Initially rejected because he had only completed the 8th grade, Joe figured that was the end of that idea. But when Fuertes found out about it, he gathered up Joe's sketches and sent them to the Institute with a strongly worded letter; Joe was accepted. He quickly sold his homestead and headed east. It was at the Art Institute of Chicago that Joe would meet his future wife and lifelong partner.

Mary Waters Cooper was born on Dec. 3, 1906 in Minneapolis, Minnesota. While still an infant, her father moved the family to Vermont. Even as a young child, Mary's interests in nature and art were evident. Her notebooks would be festooned with drawings, often of plants or animals. Her father was a member of the Green Mountain Club, which established hiking trails reaching to Canada, so Mary spent weekends hiking the hills and clearing trails. Early pictures show Mary with various animals, including several pet snakes.

Graduating from high school at the age of 16, Mary was admitted to Berea College in Kentucky. A small, prestigious school, Berea charged no tuition but required students to hold jobs at the college. When Mary arrived, she brought one of her pet snakes which caused quite a commotion and was eventually placed in the biology lab.

While Mary was at college, her family relocated to Chicago. Joining them there following graduation, she began taking classes at the Art Institute of Chicago. Classes in animal anatomy were held at the Field Museum of Natural History, and one day while Mary was sketching animals, someone walked up behind her and remarked, "That's a helluva good bear!" It was Joe Back.

Joe courted Mary during 1931 and 1932, and they finally married in February of 1933, during the great depression. Jobs were scarce, but Joe was hired as a foreman by the National Park Service for $175 a month, and Mary was appointed to run a trailside wildlife museum for $100 per month. They lived on Joe's salary and saved Mary's earnings with a plan to move to Wyoming.

In the spring of 1935, Joe and Mary bought a 1927 Buick to make the trip west. They sewed a canvas tent which could be affixed to the side of the car and camped their way through the country, arriving at Dubois, Wyoming, Joe's old stomping ground.

Moving to the high country, Mary and Joe purchased the abandoned and dilapidated Lava Creek Ranch. Working nearly round the clock, they rendered the ranch cabins ready for winter. And that first winter was a tough one with deep snow and cold temperatures. Joe would take 2 days to snowshoe the 22 miles to Dubois for the mail and a few groceries. But they both decided to stick it out.

Given her somewhat genteel and urban background, it is amazing how much Mary took to Wyoming's wildlands. Her sentiments are perfectly reflected in a short essay to the Berea College alumni newsletter, where she spoke of her first winter in the wilderness.

"Sheer beauty. It is a privilege to just be in a world so lovely, so bright with changing color; so rich in the detail of bird and animal form and action, and the patterning of the lodgepoles and the willows; so tremendous in the massing of the great mountains; so aloof and remote from the smoke and fussiness of human crowding."

Then later, "There is a relief to all one's senses at the lessened feeling of being just a cog in a great, impersonal, and intricate Society, the relief and responsibility of being "on your own" for better or for worse."

And in closing, "I have actually heard this vivid, beautiful, ever-changing country called "God-forsaken." We both find it in our hearts to thank God that it is so comparatively human-forsaken."

Mary and Joe ran the Lava Creek Ranch as a dude outfit for nearly 4 years. These were lean times, calling for improvisation and doing it yourself. Mary learned to do carpentry, dig ditches, butcher elk, and skin beaver. During the fall, Joe would be gone for weeks on end guiding hunters, and in her journals Mary speaks of how lonely she became without him; truly an inseparable pair.

They later sold Lava Creek Ranch and bought the Rocker Y, another dude ranch, but a bigger operation. While they loved the lifestyle, it did not allow them the time they needed to pursue their art careers. After a long day in the saddle or a day spent cooking and cleaning, their creative energies for painting and drawing were diminished.

During World War II, Joe and Mary worked for the war effort in California; Joe as a shipyard welder, and Mary as an airplane mechanic. Returning to Dubois at the war's end, they dude ranched for one more year.

By the spring of 1946, Joe and Mary came to realize that they would never become full-time artists running a hectic dude outfit. They sold the Rocker Y, moved east of Dubois and built a cabin that would also serve as an art studio.

Drawing and sculpting did not pay all the bills, so Joe took odd jobs, including stints with the Wyoming Game and Fish Department as a seasonal game warden and packing fish into the wilderness for stocking. He also continued guiding hunters and always got his own elk for the winter's meat - a staple since the Lava Creek days.

Joe published a small pamphlet on horse packing, "How to Tie a Diamond Hitch" illustrated with his colorful sketches. It was in big demand, so he launched a book project to produce a "horse packer's bible." The end product was *Horses, Hitches and Rocky Trails*, still in print and considered one of the best guides to horse packing in existence. His last chapters advocate respecting the wilderness and keeping care of the mountain country. He would later publish several other books, and Mary would publish *Seven Half-Miles From Home*, a reminiscence of her walks in the upper Wind River country.

The University of Wyoming asked Mary to teach extension art classes, and she was soon teaching in Dubois, Lander, Crowheart and

Riverton. Her classes were immensely popular, and the annual art show she arranged for her students and regional artists gave rise to the Wind River Valley Artists' Guild. Her efforts were later recognized when she received the Governor's Award for Service to the Arts. In addition, both she and Joe were awarded the Medallion of Honor by Central Wyoming College in 1982.

The Backs celebrated their 50th wedding anniversary in 1983, and over 200 people arrived at their small studio home. This turnout portrayed the public's appreciation for all of Joe and Mary's community service.

Joe Back passed away on September 7, 1986. This was a terrific blow to Mary - she had lost her husband, best friend, and lifelong partner in all affairs. Despite the loss, Mary continued her work with the Wind River Valley Artists' Guild and maintained her habit of walking and bird watching along the Wind River; but she had lost much of her desire to paint with Joe's passing.

Mary Back died on May 28, 1991, but the legacy of Joe and Mary Back lives on through their artwork, writings and in the fond memories of countless friends.

The Wind River Valley Artists' Guild is now housed in the beautiful Headwaters Arts and Conference Center in Dubois. Visitors can enjoy the artwork of Joe and Mary Back as well as many other fine artists.

Joe and Mary Back were inducted into the Wyoming Outdoor Hall of Fame in 2013.

—Courtesy of Wyoming Game & Fish Department

Preface

In offering this book to the public I'll admit I've stuck my neck
out; and while it's some shorter than that on Nosy the moose, it's a
gambler's neck.

Much of this story is based on actual happenings, encounters, and
life with the moose family. A few squirts of mustard and a dash or
two of applesauce have been added to enliven the proceedings.
Although the names of the human characters are wholly fictitious
and some of the incidents more than border on the imaginary, many
of them have happened to me, to my friends, and to other inhabitants
of the moose country.

As most of us are more familiar with the human than with the
deer family, it may be of interest to some to take a peek behind the
moosehide curtain.

It seems to me that the moose has had more insulting slurs cast
in his direction than any other member of his family. Beauty is only
skin deep, some say, and, brother, this critter has a thick one.

If the human, needing swamp salad, would dive down in a deep
and muddy pond or slough and grope around to snap his snout
about a lily root to have a little chew, when he came up he'd be a
little snooty, too. The moose is one of the original skin divers, with
a hair shirt on, of course. His built in air supply, nose valves, and
knowhow was developed long before his two-legged critic ever
thought of it. Maybe they stole his patent. Some moose have been
clocked to stay under for a minute and close to two.

You should see him or maybe her rare up on a tangled willow
clump to flop that rubber kisser around a thumb-thick willow. To
strip the leaves and twigs off, a beaver can't beat this slicker. He
leaves the trunk to maybe grow more next· year. And watch him
stand in snow hip deep to a tall Indian, reach up and shred the bark
off trunks of live green quaking aspen, cottonwoods, and sometimes
fir. All this with no upper teeth in front. Now he can't brag about
this too loud. The other deer are fixed the same way for upper front
teeth; except that elk and sometimes caribou do have two canines up
above; but they're too far back to do much good.

Some folks say the moose *don't eat grass*. Now some folks don't

1

stray too far from town, and when they do, they don't stay long. Mr. and Mrs. Big Nose don't eat *much* but they do eat *some*. I've watched them do it and so have many others.

And we'd get bored with the grub that nature built his insides to handle. Like us, the moose has bilious tantrums. He'll stand close up to haystacks that tease his smell and taste buds to bore large holes chest high and shoulder deep. He's after cured willow leaves, seedy twigs, timothy and wild grass heads and blossoms. The gut he's got can't stand a bender like this long, though. The bellyache he gets from this kind of digestive hangover drives him to a quick willow diet for cure; or he finally flops to become a beast for the coyotes and a dainty for the birds.

While he's taking the willow cure, let's consider some of his other peculiarities. You would think he likes music, because he wears a bell; but it never rings. His tail is too short to shoo the flies; it's just for balance. He uses bog holes and makes a wallow to knock the bugs off. His ears are long and floppy, but most times he can hear good. The moose is morose because he's near-sighted and can't wear glasses. What he lacks in humor is more than made up in temper. His legs are long and his neck is short. You've maybe seen him stand spraddle-legged, giraffe style, to try to reach the ground. In winter, tired of eating snow and scared of trappy, open, icy water holes, he'll stand on lake or river ice, to spraddle out and flop his long tongue in and out and back and forth to lick up moisture for a paunch full of soured old willow twigs. He can't help it, if his neck is nearly a half shorter than that long head he's so proud of.

He may not be nearly as articulate as his noisy cousins, the elk and the deer, but his own kind understand him. Personally, I think the moose is jealous of the elk. The elk is the most intelligent of the deer family, and the moose is afraid of him and with reason. But somebody has to be boss and it's a lot of trouble anyhow. Besides, everybody can't be foreman.

The moose, I believe, is the most primitive of the deer family, as a thinker, anyhow. That's what makes him a character. He seems to be proud of the fact that he don't know what he's going to do next and you don't either. Somebody's got to be erratic or they'll quit using the word. When he gets mad, he stands there staring straight at you, just like a mad bill collector. He'll run his tongue in and out in time with those dangerous long legs and feet stamping up and down. Just like you and me as kids. But watch *this* kid. He's about to make up his mind, if any, and you're in front.

His fastest gait is a trot. You should see him travel through deep mucky swamps, and up steep mountain sides chock full of down timber and soggy snow. When he's scared, he don't like to let on. This moose has pride. Lots of times he'll casually walk into the timber until he thinks he's out of sight, then his imagination hits him. He'll bust up through the jungle like a locoed locomotive. He probably forgot to trot, and tried to gallop or run, got his pistons all mixed up with his connecting rods, and fell down. He flusters to his feet, then he'll trot away from there.

The tracks he leaves on dry ground are sometimes hard to tell from elk tracks. Moose tracks are usually larger, longer, and pointed more than elk. But follow walking tracks for twenty yards— usually dim prints of dew-claws can finally be found. Usually means moose.

When in deep snow or mud, you're sure of moose tracks if the animal *doesn't* drag his toes much. To see this willow chomper travel in deep snow is to watch an efficient machine built for the work. He lifts his legs up, front and back, nearly vertically each step, then plunges them down rapier style for forward movement. Not much drag. He may not be compact, and he's lost his fins, but boy, the moose is a graceful machine on the job.

There have been many instances of moose pets. Some moose have been broken to harness and driven. A man sixty miles from here brought up a cow moose from a calf and used her as a trick animal on exhibition in several of the large cities. Her end was tragic, as with lots of other pets. Some brave jackass hunter shot her for a trophy close to her home shed in a settled district.

Here's a lot to the moose and a little to the men. When next you see a moose I hope you'll remember little Nosy. And I also hope you like this book.

So long,
Joe Back
Dubois, Wyoming.

The Bird Watchers

It was fall, and many birds were flocking together to make plans and dates for migration to warmer climes. A bird watchers group from the Nature Club was having a picture contest and bird list race. George Takum and his hefty mate, off on a lone trip, were way ahead in the contest.

Nosy had taken a much needed dietary vacation from his lunches on handouts and sometimes filched provisions. He'd had a change of food in the past week of roaming the timbered expanses above Bill Thompson's ranch. Now on his way home, his stomach adjusted for a new campaign, he had spotted the big car on the hill road, and was modestly hid in the nearby willows shyly surveying these interesting humans just getting out of their car.

George Takum was the junior member of the Casem, Loanum, and Takum Investment Company, and was on his way up. Having finally acquired title to several ranches in an oh, so sorry, way, Takum felt that any wild game around was his for the taking—especially because he had seen members of the deer family grazing in the meadows of his several ranches at odd times. The pious-looking loan shark felt that fair exchange was no robbery. Of course, one had to discreetly observe the proprieties. The Game Department men had to do their jobs, of course, to keep down the hungry appetites of the nearby ne'er-do-well ranchers and the local riffraff natives. Although Jayne genteely frowned on these wicked little habits of her Gawge, she had to admit privately that she got a distinctly peculiar thrill whenever her clever provider brought home some illicit bacon—especially when she met the game warden or his wife on the streets of Roaring River.

"Ouh, Gawge, my deah," her Grim Mahwr accent had commando undertones, but hearing no "Yayus, Jayne, muh love," didn't bother this militant stage managuh of the Little Theatuh. She couldn't take her bulging eyes away from her Bird Watchuh Specials for fear of losing sight of the rare bird. The lady firmly held the binoculars in a be-ringed grip. George had stopped to tighten up a loose lace on his boots on the steep hillside just below the car. He thought he'd seen a moose calf down in the swamp below the road. His big calibre,

"The Go Git 'Em Special" he called it, was in the back seat of the station wagon within easy reach.

After calling several times to her husband to hurry up and identify the bird she'd spotted, the angry stage manager lowered her glasses and turned around. There was the investment counselor kneeling down in the tall yellow grass, his ought-six rifle aimed down the hill. She turned her powerful glasses on just what tidbit Old Thrifty had located now. Bill Thompson's little brown milk cow had gotten out of the pasture. The grazing Jersey never will find out that she owed her bovine life to the main member of the Little Theater Group. Jayne caught the sound of Annie's bell, and from her different point of vantage, saw that Takum's avarice had gone just a little too far. When her shrill yell of warning reached the slightly deaf loan man, he had taken up the slack on old Go-Git-Em's trigger. But he took his itchy finger away in irritation at the yowling of the bird watcher. A fat moose calf was just what the doctor ordered, and so Gawge was peeved.

Popeyed, George stood staring down the hillside at the Jersey cow now moving into the open, her clanging bell audible now even to the chagrined hunter.

"If you'll put that nasty old gun back into the cah, I'll try to locate that bird again," Jayne fumed at Old Dead-Eye. "I'll declah, trying to kill a poor little old Jersey cow."

"I'll swear, Jayne, that was the first time I've ever seen a fat moose calf turn into a milk cow." Takum looked back down the hillside as he put his disappointed rifle in the big station wagon. The line of willows bordering the swiftly falling creek looked innocent enough, as the little brown Jersey grazed out of sight behind a stand of timber.

"You should know there's no moose within miles of heah at this time of yeah." The irate bird watcher walked over towards her original stand and was again trying to spot the strange bird. Watching the antics of this couple, the hidden bog trotter had decided that they weren't worth his while, when the wind shifted. The smell of Big Money nauseated the calf, but the scent Mrs. Money Bags used was intensely interesting. So Nosy trotted out of the willows straight for Mrs. Takum, who was snooping through her B.W. Specials in the other direction. Gawge T. was disgustedly walking over to his beckoning mate when he heard the grunting mutters of the long-nosed customer on his way over to the new perfume counter.

The single-minded calf, seeing Takum's hurried and speechless ascent of a nearby pine out of the corner of an eye, was now up close to the interesting lady in the well-filled pants. Jayne Takum mistook the pleased whines behind her for her helpmate's usual smothered comments. Keeping her eyes grimly fixed on the pretty birdie, impatiently she held the leather loop high in one hand, and the field glasses ready for her tall husband's confirmation in the other.

Takum himself had by now got his wind back. Seeing the pot-bellied pet about to look through those expensive binoculars, he couldn't take it. He howled a frenzied warning at the waiting bird woman. When the investment counselor's wife whipped her head around, to meet the softly affectionate gaze of the short-tailed party of the third part, she gave a theatrical screech and dived into the nearest haven of safety, the huge shell of an ancient fire-killed tree lying close by.

Old Lady Badger had found what she considered the ideal nursing home. The hollow-end log was long dead, but the still thick shell extended inward four or five feet until the interior ended in a blank wall. She lay on her back at joyful ease, while her three fat babies lunched at their leisure. When Mrs. Takum went calling, she usually was more polite and rang the bell, but this time was a little different. Mrs. Badger got kind of ringy, to say the least, at Jayne's unceremonious entrance. She bared her teeth and hissed that no painted up hussy can come into my home and show me how to raise my kids.

Nosy, in his short life, had been handed a lot of odd things, mostly edible. This gift that dangled under his chin was kind of bothersome, but the moose was polite and didn't ask the reason why. When he tried to follow his new-found friend into her hollow tree for better acquaintance, his formal education started with his lady friend kicking him on the snoot on her way out.

When Jayne Takum came galloping backward out of Snuffy Badger's unfriendly apartment, the calf moose sensed an unwelcome attitude in the gathering. He whirled around and trotted off into the heavy timber. He didn't even notice that the descending junior member of Casem, Loanum, and Takem was again on his way up.

Tony Belknap had spent a few hours visiting with Velma and Bill Thompson, and was now untying his saddle horse from the backyard fence. His two friends were saying their so longs, when Nosy walked out from around the corner of the corral. As Bill and his wife stood staring at the calf, Tony hurriedly stepped on his

7

He howled a frenzied warning.

horse and started to ride off. They could hear the startled cowboy mumble, "By gravy, Ol' Bill's shore slipped his pack. Furnishin' that damn near-sighted pest with a pair uh glasses! Wait till *this* gits around. *By hell, I've seen everything* now!"

Hay Stealer

Whoa, now, I'm getting a little ahead of the story about that little moose. Maybe it would be better to start at the beginning of what happened, that early winter at the head of Roaring River. The hunting camp and gear were all packed into the ranch. Most of the pack and saddle horses had been driven below town on winter pasture. The two men put in a wood camp a few miles above the ranch to get out logs and firewood till deep snow stopped their operations. Up to now, things had been going pretty good. Snow was getting deeper up high in the mountains, and more moose were showing up.

This one stamped her feet in a sort of crazy dance and kept time with her tongue running in and out of her mouth. The coarse mane rising upon her short neck and the "I'll gitcha" look rolling in her near-sighted eyes completed the picture for Tony Belknap. He gave a scrambling hop off the sled-load of logs and plowed through the deep snow for the nearest stand of spruce.

Bill Thompson calmly see-sawed the leather lines on his team of roans who were trying to jacknife the front bob in the deeply rutted snow. He wrapped the lines around the chain boomer handle, reached into the canvas nose-bag he kept tied to the binding chain, and came out with a slingshot and a rock. Ignoring the stomping of the cow moose ahead, he let fly at a clump of willows in back of her. There was a surprised squeal from a big calf, hit dead center. The ungainly mamma whirled around with a grunt and plunged off, with her gangling offspring trailing along in her wake.

Tony plowed sheepishly back to the bobsled. Bill bit off a fresh chew and said, "OK, sissy, git on 'n' we'll go t' camp. Ain't yuh never seen a locoed cow moose before? Yu' only been around 'em for sixty years!"

"Yuh dumb wrinkled-up ol' fool," barked Tony as he bowlegged up behind Bill, "them Mizzouri tricks'll git you killed yet. You an' that crazy bean-shooter!"

"Aw, hell," says Bill, and pops the team on the rumps with a loud yell, "why don't you get modern? These rock-throwers is plenty handy t'have around, don't hurt a thing."

They saw one more moose as they stopped the team on the brink of a steep hill just above camp. While they put the roughlock chains on the back runners, Tony kept a wary eye on the bull as he crunched the crowns off small green spruce and lodgepole trees. When they clambered back up on the load of dry logs and started the team down the drop-off, the screeching of chain-bound steel on snow and rocks made the big moose take off, trotting smoothly in the direction of Bill's camp on Mosquito Creek.

"Damn him," says Bill. "Didja see that hay stickin' up there, tangled in his mane?"

"A sign he's one o' yer nosy friends, I reckon," says Tony. "You sure take up with some onery lookin' characters."

"Well, by hell, if you went 'n' left those poles down when you hitched up t' the sled this mornin', some o' that forty-dollar hay'll be comin' outa yer wages, my big-hatted friend." Bill slapped angrily with the lines to hurry up the horses.

Down in the next park they took off the roughlock chains and drew up in front of the rickety buzz saw and truck engine Bill swore by and at. The small cook shack looked intact. The corral looked okay at first glance, but as they started to unhook the team, a roaring grunt warned them. Bill held on to the plunging team as a huge moose dashed past them, with a mass of baling wire tangled up in his horns and around a bunged-up front leg. When Tony came out from behind a standing tree, he says, "If this ain't a hay-wire outfit, I'll put in with yuh!"

While Tony led the horses over to the creek for a drink, Bill hurried over to the hay corral—four trees he'd nailed poles to. The gate poles were up, all right, and the baling wire loops that held them were intact. But a couple other poles were knocked down, lying on the snow covered ground, the big spikes still in the ends. The moose, pushing hard to grab at the precious bales of tasty native hay, had finally made the grade. Bill always hung the wire from the bales on a tree limb for emergency repairs, thus unconsciously setting a trap for four-legged thieves. But the trap was sprung after the bait was eaten.

Whenever he got enough ahead, Thompson would haul logs to his ranch and firewood to town twenty miles below the wood camp. Every time he hauled wood to his customers, he would haul grub and hay back up. The hay had a lot of cured willow leaves and stems and other native seeds and grass mixed up in it.

The moose population, weary of the early heavy snows and bored

11

by their natural diet of willows, bark, and other forest tidbits, had taken to raiding Bill's hard-won horse feed. They wasted more than they ate while searching for what they could digest. Their natural erratic behavior was making the two loggers uneasy.

"They kinda resent us birds invadin' their private domain," Bill remarked to Tony. "Y're dead right, partner," Tony had just about his fill of moose. "Them dang critters also don't know whut they're goin' t' do next and we don't either."

He unharnessed and fed the horses while Bill nailed the poles back up to the trees, and reenforced the spikes by twisting wire around trees and poles.

"Winter's sure early," Tony grunted as he hung his hat over his coat on the inside of the cookshack door, and pulled off his head the wool sock that protected his ears. "Huh," Bill was loading the stove with kindling and striking a match, "Yuh wouldn't feel th' cold if y'd wear a Scotch cap 'n' quit tryin' ta be a cowboy fashion plate." He bent down to the wood box, rammed the door with his head, and knocked it open. Out into the dark rolled Tony's precious headgear, and out leaped Tony to its rescue. Bill shook his head and stoked up the stove.

After supper Bill rolled the logs off the bobsled onto the skids by his saw rig. He hobbled the horses, put a bell on old Dick, and turned them loose for the night. He knew they'd be right there at the hay corral for breakfast next morning. He re-piled the bales of hay in the center of the little corral, and raked up the scattered leavings of a broken bale with a pitchfork. He leaned the pitchfork against a tree trunk, and crunched over to his truck for a few blocks of sawed wood to split for the breakfast fire. As he stacked it handy by the shack, Tony, who'd washed the supper dishes, unhooked the door and threw the dishwater out on the trod-down snow just outside. Bill looked up and said, " 'Ja bring yer skates, Tony?" No answer. Tony was too busy wrangling the dishpan, catching his hat in the air, and getting it back on the nail, all at the same time.

In the dim light of frosty morning, Bill woke to hear the horse bell's loud clanging. He prodded Tony back to cold reality from his dream of a big ranch and many cows. After he got dressed, he opened the door and stepped out—to put one shoe-pack square in Tony's big hat, the other on the frozen dishwater. At his loud skiddy fall, the horses and Tony all showed up, to see him brushing snow and profane anger all over the cowhand's messed-up hat and the echoing timbered landscape. Tony was grieving loudly as he started the breakfast fire, while the bruised logger haltered the two horses and tied them up to the corral poles. He hung the hobbles on a tree limb, and was just reaching up to unbuckle the bell strap from Dick's frosty neck, when he heard a musty belch. He looked over the poles directly into the unbeautiful face of a willow-cruncher with a half flake of cured willow leaves and native hay crosswise in his mouth. All of a sudden Bill lost his philosophy of "share-the-wealth". He grabbed the pitchfork by the handle, aimed its sharp business end at the boarder, and gave a forty-dollar lunge at the moose's flopping smeller. In just about a tenth of a second, a mess of tangled-up broken poles, hungry horses, scared logger, and murderous moose were headed hell-bent in the same busy direction. Hare-lipped now and dripping blood, the hay-stealer cut Bill out from the small and frantic horse herd with a deadly precision that amazed cowboy Tony, watching the show from the open shack door. Big hat tipped on one side of his head, he stepped closer to see the sights better. The moose had Bill all lined up and was closing in to make the deal final.

There was no affection in the moose's passionate breath on his neck. Bill didn't stop to check with his compass but speeded up in a desperate scrawly rush for the shack and solid shelter. Seeing the parade approach, Tony turned too fast, slipped, and fell ka-phump on the frozen dishwater and lost his big hat in the snow banked up nearby. He just made the door in time and yanked it shut in a hurry. Bill, at a high lope, howled, "Open th' door, yuh damn' sap, this moose ain't a-foolin!"

The fat was in the fire—Tony had backed up too far while holding the door shut. When he felt the fiery sizzling on his rump from the booming cook stove, he thought the moose must have come in through the back window. So he kicked the door open, and made a running jump to, he hoped, safety. He and Bill collided, and Tony fell underneath. Bill's eyes were blinded by the spurting snowy rush of Tony's exit. He thought he was on top of the cantankerous moose, and grabbed for his mane, but all he got was a mane holt on Tony's shaggy black hair. The moose had missed his aim at poor wind-broken old Bill. He stepped right into the cowboy's waiting hat and poured on speed straight up the logging road. Distant moggy coughs told of his fears of the Stetson trap now flopping just below a hock.

The two worn-out loggers sorted out who was who, and at last were painfully gulping hot coffee in the shack. Tony was sadly

A mess of tangled-up poles, hungry horses, scared logger, and murderous moose.

figuring how many cords of sawed wood it took to buy a new hat. Bill gave old Bowlegs a long, hard look, and says, "Why in hell didja shut that door?" Tony felt of the burned place under his singed wool pants, and yelped, "Why, yuh danged ol' coot, there wa'n't room fer three of us in here!"

15

The Water Bucket

The deep snows came early. They kept piling up so bad that Bill and Tony had to pull up stakes and call it quits. With truck and bobsled they got the whole outfit hauled down to the ranch. Tony got a job shoveling hay for a cow outfit. Bill planned to put in the rest of the winter building a log barn on his own place.

Moose showed up early in the bottoms along Roaring River, glad for the shelter and food in the miles of willow jungle. You could see them every mile or two—groups of four or five cows and calves, sometimes solitary old bulls or grumpy cows enjoying their own company. You could see those snouty swamp-lovers, in groups or singly, breath steaming, standing up and reaching high, to snap their pendulous upper lips around the succulent stems of the head-high ropy growths. The deep snow served as beds and generous water supply.

With a huge thumbnail Bill scraped some of the frost away from a window and peered out over the willow flats below the hill. No moose in sight. The leaden sky was just beginning to lighten up Bull Ridge, the timber covered hill crowding the far side of Roaring River.

Bill's wife, Velma, was bustling around the humming kitchen range, getting set for breakfast. She was full of pep and impatient with Ol' Bill. He was taking turns looking out the scratched streaks of window and staring glumly at the two new galvanized pails he'd brought back from town, ten snow-coverd miles away.

"Well, if you want any breakfast *this* morning, you'd better get a hump on, and go fetch a couple buckets of water. I'm tired of melting snow," Velma said, putting a fresh stick of wood in the stove.

Bill quit scraping peep holes in the frosty glass and warmed his cold thumb by adjusting his new store teeth. He reached up for his ragged wool coat on a nail behind the door, mumbling, "OK, but you'd better keep the dumb dog in here. I've got sore bumps all over me from yesterday." The beautiful white collie, safe behind the wood box, sniffed in the direction of the frozen slab of elk meat Velma was sawing at. His long patrician nose wrinkled with disdain at Bill's voice.

"If you'd be a little considerate of Moocher," Velma pointed

16

Bill's hunting knife in his direction, "he'd be more considerate of you. Besides, he's only a pup. He's just growing up. That's what his papers said. About his age."

"Yeah, and what a pup! That fancy-pants brother of yours told me the strawberry roan he traded me for that load of logs is young, too. I looked in his mouth—he's been four years old for ten years anyhow."

Bill limped over to the table, grabbed the new pails, and started for the door, favoring his sore leg. The spring water supply had failed—the water froze up in the shallow pipe system before Bill got it shut off. The spring creek flowing from the timbered mountain up behind the cabins would freeze and thaw and terrace up in frozen knobs and boils. The day before Moocher had brushed Bill off an icy plank at the spring, chasing a snowshoe rabbit who played daily games with the useless warrior.

Mittens and Scotch cap in place, old Bill warily opened the door. Just before he got it jerked shut behind him, Moocher flashed past him and out. Bill was thrown into the cross chains of a log sled just outside the door. The heavy snow muffled his curses and the sounds of flying pails, but cushioned his fall. Moocher was chasing a weasel. Its black tail tip flipped in derision as it disappeared under the log storehouse.

Bill got up, wordless now in the gathering light. He gave an angry glance back at the cabin, but its closed door was no help. He found the pails and started plowing through the fresh snow, past the gloomy deserted summer cabins. As his feet felt for the snow-filled trail, his eyes automatically looked for stray moose in the willows on each side of his path. Near the river he looked up the trail to the cowshed and corral, thinking he ought to have given the little Jersey more hay last night.

Moose tracks were everywhere, criss-crossed through the deep snow from one dense willow clump to the next. Hummocks and dead willow roots made it rough country for walking, down here where the river's roar sounded from the water hole, where the frosty mist smoked up from the dark rushing water. Trotting warily along, Bill wished he'd worn his sheepskin coat. His loose teeth chattered in time with his shivering limbs. The intense cold was eating its way in under the ragged henskin jacket. Bad footing here; glassy from spilled water. No animals in sight among the willows of the jungly cafeteria; but some melted beds showed where they'd been.

Bill set his pails down to get a good look around before filling them.

17

These willows had seen foot-races before, Bill so far staying the winner. Now he wished he'd slung his trusty '06 on his back. Just as he started to kneel down on the ragged edge of the chopped-out water hole, he tottered on the slick ice and nearly fell in—Moocher had arrived in a snowy rush, just brushing the hillbilly's pants as he passed. Scared and enraged, the water packer stood and wildly informed the snowy landscape of his very low opinion of the collie and his alleged pedigree. Moocher, meanwhile, white tail proudly high, was gaily disappearing down the river on a moose trail.

Bill hurriedly knelt down again. As the rushing water filled his pail, he jerked it up and set it brimming on a flat place on the slippery trail. The bail of the bucket stood upright, frozen into place. Another shivering look around, and old Bill grabbed the other pail and quickly bent down.

Just as the furious water yanked at it, he heard a ki-yi-yi-ing of desperate come-help-me anguish. He looked up to see Velma's registered pride and joy flying to him for protection, with a big bull moose close behind. The pail made a choked clatter as the river grabbed it, and Bill took off, waiting for no formal introduction. Believing in straight lines, he pounded his packs toward the closer cow's corral and safer quarters. A cold hollowness inside him promoted record time. The mighty Moocher left a trail of woeful wails up the longer trail toward the cabins.

The moose quickly transferred his hostile intentions and now wanted to get acquainted with the water packer. But as he swerved to his new course he saw the bucket and plowed to a stop, his big toes and dewclaws raising a cloud of snow. He snorted and blew through his bulbous smeller at the thing in his way. Nothing moved. He pawed, then hooked at the bucket. As he brought up his antlers, the long brow tine on one side hooked into the waiting bail. Bill's reprieve was over; the jar broke the surface ice on the filled pail; it cracked like a gun. Old Snooty took off in a hurry after the mountain man. Poor Ol' Bill heard the whanging and banging of metal and horn, but about that time he didn't feel curious. Just short of the corral, he skidded to a hard fall. The cow trail dipped down and over the deep ruts of Bill's sled road to timber. There Bill sprawled in a frantic wrestle with frosty gravity.

Up came the moose, full speed ahead, muttering querulous grunts at the tinny rattling. One eye was hidden by icicles and hoarfrost, the other rolled in a vicious calculation. But he was off a little on windage and elevation, for he missed the scrambling man by a yard.

He was off a little on windage and elevation.

Bill got up and galloped up to and over the corral in one frantic surge of speed. He'd had a cold canine start, but his arrival was a race-horse finish. He sounded like a wind-broken Caruso.

His pet, the little milk cow, was bedded down in the open-faced shed, chewing her cud in sleepy comfort, when she was thus rudely interrupted. Her rest had been disturbed by nightly observations by curious moose peepers, and now, by alfalfa, here they were again, and in the daytime!

She got up in a furious Jersey tantrum, sharp curved horns down. With an unladylike bellow, her bell clanging, she charged out of the flimsy shed at the first thing she saw, poor old sweating and heaving Bill. This was Bill's second race. He scrambled for the highest corral pole. It wasn't high enough, and the moose belched willowy blasts into his face. So Thompson raced around inside, pursued by the bellowing Jersey, while the moose raced outside. He got the pail dislodged and stomped it into a tinny mess. His squealing roars kept encouraging the Jersey.

Bill finally made a damn-near-too-late Orville Wright to the top of the shed. In the race, he'd lost his Scotch cap and a mitten. As he jumped, he hoped that the slight loss of weight would be enough to keep him from going through the flimsy roof.

He tried to sweet-talk the Jersey into remembering him. The moose stopped to listen. Through with her moose-mare, the cow finally calmed down and let Bill get off the roof.

He was getting chillier and chillier, chattering and shaking with cold. When he pulled the jacket up to warm his cold head, his back was exposed. He tried to put both hands into one mitten, with no luck. The bull moose just stayed there, re-stomping the battered bucket, making muttering squeals at the corral. Bill shouted and hollered for Velma, with no luck so far. The cabin was west of the corrals, and the wind was wrong. A heavy stand of timber muffled the sounds of his hoarse calls for help.

Yelping up the cabin trail, Moocher was stopped by the closed door. Sure that Bill was in a tantrum at some prank of her pet, Velma let him in. She gave him some milk, and went on mixing up flapjacks for the three of them. By now she began to get worried about Bill. She put on her heavy coat and her overshoes and went out into the bitter Wyoming weather, with Moocher along for protection.

First she went to the brink of the hill to look toward the waterhole. She yelled and yelled and peered through frost-rimmed eyelids down at the clusters of willows. No sign of Bill, but her screaming intrigued

20

the remaining lodge brothers of Ol' Bill's big bull moose. Seeing those dark big ears coming into sight, Velma remembered how Bill, a member of the Elks, said the B.P.O.E. had the Moose skinned all to thunder. She became alarmed, thinking Bill was mebbe being initiated into an order he detested. Moocher barked to the universe. The west wind carried the barks and yells down to the corral.

Velma remembered the corral. She retraced her steps to the cabin, then went eastward on the bobsled tracks till she could see out of the timber to the corral and shed below. At first, in the numbing cold, she could see nothing but a moose moving slowly round the outside of the snowy corral, and the Jersey inside. She was just about to turn back when the wind died down, and Bill managed to turn loose one last loud yowl for help. The Jersey, startled, shook her head, and her bell set up a hollow bonging. Moocher dodged Velma's fingers and dashed down the hill, looking for an exhilarating cow chase.

Velma trotted bravely down the frozen ruts, her fear of moose overcome by her love of the dog. The moose looked up when he heard her shrill calls, and saw the small red-coated figure and the spurting gusts of Moocher-driven snow. He gave a weird rolling snort and took off at a swinging trot for the heavy timber, his long hairy bell dangling sidewise in the wind.

Bill had only a hoarse greeting of "That blamed dog." Velma gasped angrily, "Why, you old stoop, he saved your life, and you still run him down!"

Crouched by the roaring fire in the stove, Bill gradually thawed out. Velma poured coffee and set out breakfast. Now in a more genial frame of mind, Bill even gave the collie a furtive grin. But when he started to eat the tender and fragrant elk steaks, he let out a howl of frustration. "What in the world is biting you now?" asked Velma, surprised and angry.

Bill choked out, "It's me, biting this elk meat! Now it ain't only that confounded collie and no water pails, but where in hell are my new store teeth?"

Innocent Hell-Raiser

Bill pulled up the team, with only another hundred yards to go. "Danged if the chain didn't slip off again. Better not take a chance. These horses are still spooky from them moose last winter." He kept a tight hold on the lines, and walked over to tie on to a standing tree beside the rocky skid trail. The load was a light one—some poles for the buck fence he was building—but he'd been hauling plenty of them this spring. The tired rancher mused, "If I don't see another blamed bog-trotter in a hundred years, that'd be too soon."

Ol' Bill took the chain off the doubletrees and wrapped a couple hitches around the pile of long poles. He got the slide hook adjusted. He was about to hook into the clevis on the doubletrees when the team of roans lunged ahead, snorting their fright at something coming out of the willows along the creek below the skid trail. Bill saw that the tied lines stopped the jittery horses, and looked around. There was a long-legged moose calf staggering up out of the rocky creek. His reddish coat was splotched with mud, and the eyes in his homely big head were half shut. A long gash on one of his knobby hind legs was sticky with half-dried blood.

The logger put his big hands over his eyes and moaned, "Oh, not again, oh, no! All winter long, and here's one o' th' dang babies come to gimme hell." As he stared at the short-backed, long-legged infant of the swampy jungles, the ugly little fellow gave a weak whine and fell down, right at Bill's unwilling feet. Now, you couldn't fool ol' Bill, not with this kind of "Come on, sucker" play. He knew that maw was handy, and when a mama moose mislays her baby there's hell to pay. Bill didn't feel like paying any bills, not then, and not to any damn moose. He knew that moosenapping is a dang sight more dangerous than kidnapping. He was about to leave those poles and take him and the horses to a safer place as of now. "Damn the snooty things, anyhow." Then Bill furiously untied the lines and drove the anxious horses at a trot further up into heavier timber. He looked back down at the dense growth of willows. There was no movement except the moose calf trying weakly to regain his feet. Bill took down the halter ropes and tied the snuffy team to a big tree. He decided he had to see what the mystery was.

"I ain't too old t' climb a tree," he mumbled to himself, "but mebbe I won't have ta." He looked cautiously in all directions as he walked down through the trees. He made a sneaky circle through the jungle of willows, crossed the roaring creek on a handy log, and was about to head back toward the moose calf, when he saw a couple of ravens fly up out of a clump of small spruce just below him. He went to look and came on the dead body of a huge cow moose. Her hind leg was trapped in a snaky loop of a tree root. The broken leg, the torn up earth and rocks, the peeled bark on the spruce told the story of a futile battle. Now it looked like her forlorn heir still had hopes there must be friends somewhere in these hills.

Bill paused just to look at the starved swamp baby. But when the ugly calf swayed suddenly to his feet and grabbed Bill's fingers to start sucking, the hillbilly knew he was lost.

"I don't give a hoot what Velma says," Bill tells the wall-eyed little starveling, "a feller can't let ambition like this go to waste." With a bunch of green branches tied on to the poles with one halter rope, and the struggling orphan tied to this bed with another, Bill skidded the whole wooden ambulance right down in front of the cabin.

Velma was making butter in her new churn, but when she heard the snorting horses and dragging poles she came out on the back porch. There followed exclamations, valiant struggles by the moose, explanations, and then a bottle of milk. During its administration, Velma delivered her ultimatum on the whole moosey deal. "Now, Bill, as soon as this poor little rascal is able t' fend for himself, you'll have to run him off. From what I've seen of all your pets so far, if you don't, he'll try t' run us off before he's done. You've had 'em in your hair all winter, and now you bring one right inta the house. Looks like you don't feel natural 'thout a moose bein' close around."

In a week or so, it looked like Nosy would make it. Velma and Bill figured out some kind of a milk formula that seemed to agree with him. "Maybe it's un-Christian, but I'm afraid he's going t' live," Velma said to Bill one day, when Moocher the collie got kicked in the ribs for taking a jealous nip at the calf. "He's gotta defend himself, ain't he? If Moocher bit you on the rump, what would you do?" asked Bill, rubbing Nosy's big head.

The bull calf and Moocher made up. They would romp around like a couple of kids. But Nosy hated the cat and would vainly try to stomp on Tabby with his sharp toes. He didn't like strangers. Any who came visiting caused him to hide behind Velma or Bill, mane hair straight up, and even the hairy fringe on his sharp little rump standing

23

Bill paused just to look at the starved swamp baby.

Velma and Bill figured out a milk formula.

The bull calf and moocher made up.

Velma was showered with flapjacks.

erect. He began to figure he was the most important one in the family. He would come like a dog when he was called. He learned to pry his way into the kitchen and would sprawl on Velma's linoleum looking for handouts of celery leaves or other vegetable tidbits. She drove him out so many times he finally quit trying that. He grew fast. By the end of July he began to change color. His reddish brown started to become a grayish black on the body, and his legs up to the knees and hocks turned grayish white. He got into so many jackpots and caused so much trouble that both Bill and Velma began to wish they'd never seen him. "Adolescent moose get teen-aged a swamp sight quicker'n kids do," said Velma one day. Bill, who had suffered that time, said, "You mean a damn sight."

One morning Velma put some sourdough pancakes out for Moocher. The moose calf happened by, chased the dog off, and gobbled the cakes down. The busy housewife in the kitchen thought she heard a far-off train whistle and ran out the door to see how civilization could have got there that fast. There stood the ungainly swamp angel with his first case of hiccups. His short body was bunched together on those extra long legs, and his round belly was going like a blacksmith's bellows. He had his ears back, and his bell-shaped snoot high in the air, snuffling like a wind-broken horse. Ol' Bill was starting to saddle a horse in front of the barn when he heard Velma yelling. That was when Bill really got in the doghouse, for he came running up to the long-snouted calliope and brought down a heavy saddle blanket ka-whompie on the heaving calf's back. That stopped the hiccups in a hurry. But poor Velma, standing unstrategically in front of the bull calf, was showered with her own damp flapjacks.

Moocher came out from under the safe porch in a yelping hurry to bite the belcher on the hind leg. Nosy's kick missed the collie, but Bill got it on his belt buckle. As the moose was growing fast, being fed on things people say moose don't eat, that was a hefty punch. When Mr. Thompson got his wind back, _he_ had the hiccups, but that didn't keep him from whacking the disillusioned bull calf clear across the creek. The coughing man realized this was a huskier baby than he'd thought. His belly hurt.

No Butter on Sunday

"The minister and his new city wife are coming up for dinner, Bill." Velma was pulling fresh loaves from the hot oven. "Now, this is Sunday, and I don't want them to think we are heathens even if we are hillbillies. So if you can, just for once, keep that so-called pet of yours out of the way, maybe we can have a peaceful day." She had just got a new hairdo yesterday and felt as chipper as she looked.

Bill said he'd put the calf moose in the new horse corral just back on the barn. So he got some watercress from the fenced-in spring and tolled his bulb-nosed pet down to the corral. Next chore was the Jersey. She'd somehow got out of the cow corral last night, gathered up her calf, newly broken to drink, and hadn't shown up to be milked. As Bill saddled up a horse to ride the big meadow in search of her, he saw the moose calf still peacefully chewing watercress in the horse corral, and Velma was in sight, bustling around, sweeping the back porch. The horse snapped into a fast trot when Bill popped him with the reins. As he rode off, the thought occurred to him, "Mebbe that dang moose *is* gettin' t' be kind of a halfway pest at that. The blame thing *is* kind of rambunctious." Now, some pets are gentle and all lovey-dovey; Bill Thompson thought his moose was, but then he was bunkhouse raised, you might say. As a guide, packer, and mountain rancher, his ideas were a little basic and down-to-earth. Ol' Bill believed that Nature was gentle, if you understood just what was natural with some of Nature's children.

Everything was percolating just right, Velma thought, as she watched through a window in her trim kitchen. She could see part of the road down past the lodgepole pines and expected the minister and his wife to show up on it. "Better get fresh eggs for the cake icing," she thought, and left the kitchen and walked down the path to the log barn. She found six or eight in the manger. On her way back she went to check the long-legged menace in the horse corral. She opened the gate and saw Nosy asleep in the shadow cast by the barn. She had trouble with the pole slide lock on the gate but thought it was OK. Then she started round the barn for the house.

A new red jeep was just chugging up the road. So Velma hurried up, went in the kitchen to put the eggs away, looked in the mirror on

29

the wall to put any stray locks in place. Then she dashed to the front door, just in time to welcome the tall and smiling minister and his very dainty and feminine little wife. Velma noticed the new jeep roll forward slightly, then stop, a front wheel against a large pebble. After she'd made her visitors comfortable in the living room, Velma excused herself to put dinner on the table, saying Bill would show up soon. "Our Jersey strayed off and Bill's gone to find her. He should be here now."

As she went to the springhouse she saw Bill unsaddle his horse at the barn. The cow and her calf were in the corral gently nosing each other.

The ambitious calf moose must have pushed open the corral gate right after Velma thought she'd fastened it. In the course of his survey of what's new he saw the jeep. He had a violent dislike of any stranger or strange thing, so he smelled this suspicious object, gave a few angry squeals, backed off, and then rammed the machine into movement. As the jeep started slowly ahead, he figured that's that, the durned thing's leaving. So he trotted around the cabin just in time to see Velma leaning in the door of the springhouse. Velma had reached past some crocks of cream half immersed in the cold water to get a jar of butter, when Nosy, playfully asking for attention, gave her a very firm affectionate nudge with his big head.

Bill had decided to milk the Jersey out before he went to the house, so there he sat, with his head in her brown flank, milking away at a great rate. The peace of the Sabbath and of Bill's mind were soon shattered by the most hideous sounds ever heard on this mountain ranch. Suddenly, with deadly precision, the gentle little Jersey kicked old Bill in his unsuspecting and empty belly with one set of hooves, then rammed another set, jack-hammer style, in the nearly full pail of rich milk. The poor wrinkled-up old milkmaid sat down hard and lay back on his elbows, slathered from stem to stern, while the cow ran bellering over to the calf bawling through the corral bars. And here came his moose pet desperately whining for help. He was in a fast trot, with Velma beating on his numbed differential with a ripped-off 2x4 studded with rusty nails. The air vibrated with hideous imprecations. Bill Thompson was startled by the sudden knowledge that women can swear without cussing.

Velma's Sunday dress was all streaked and blobbed with rich Jersey cream, and her hairdo was buttered up, Mongolian style. The mountain stillness of the sunny Sabbath was punctuated with, "Either that horrible bat-brained moose has gotta go or I do, *and* it's not go-

30

The Jersey kicked Ol' Bill.

31

Gently nosing his milky overalls.

ing to be *me,* I can tell you *that!* Mr. 'Oh! he's just an innocent animal!' *Blah!* So *there!"*

A tinny crash of metal and tinkling glass in front of the cabin brought the moose- and cow-smeared pardners up there in a stumbling run, just as the tall minister and his new bride came out of the front door at an undignified trot. There was the new jeep in the rocks of the tumbling stream, with its proud red front in a pile of snaggy driftwood. As the four people gazed down together, Bill felt the huge nose of his innocent pet gently nosing his milky overalls.

Salad Days

Things weren't always at a crisis. Nosy, the pest, would disappear for a week or so at a time on business of his own. Velma was relieved, but Bill, though he wouldn't admit it, sort of missed the trouble-maker. One day he was down the road putting new poles in a section of buck fence where a falling tree had wrecked it. Some cattle passed him. When the cowboy driving them saw Bill, he got off his horse and came over to visit. It was Tony Belknap. No sooner had they howdyed and started passing news of the mountains when out of the timber came Bill's bog trotter. He walked up behind his friend, rubbed up against him, and stood glaring and snuffling at the startled cowhand.

Tony, taking no chances, hopped on his snorting pony and backed him away. "Well, I'll be damned. After all the hell them things gave yuh, yuh had ta take one in ta raise. Man, are you bushed!" Tony grunted, staring at the raised mane and laid-back ears. As he reined his horse around to leave, he sent a parting shot, "Tell Velma t' quit feedin' yuh willows!" Bill grinned and threw an arm over Nosy's withers.

The moose had disappeared another time, when Bill stopped his old pickup in the yard. Velma came out of the house and picked up the box of groceries Bill had brought from town, while he headed for the woodpile. She carefully set the grub down on the porch chair and started to open the kitchen door. She heard a crispy crunch behind her and turned to see the long stem end of her precious celery just going down Nosy's big maw. That was too much for Velma. She galloped off the porch and grabbed the nearest weapon handy, a garden rake. The young bull with the longest nose on Roaring River dodged, but not fast enough. Velma was raking his gray rump with every step. If you don't think ranch women can run and holler at the same time, you should have seen this race. Moocher, tagging along behind, enjoyed it, but Nosy didn't. In the short time it took the speeding moose to get to the woodpile, the ferocious housewife had a crossword puzzle pattern engraved in red furrows on the robber's back. Velma's fellow members of the church guild would have been

34

Velma was raking his gray rump.

dismayed to hear the descriptive comments that came down with every vicious stroke of their chairman's weapon.

Bill Thompson, the alleged head of the house, had ten good toes, but nearly lost half of them when his falling axe missed the block of wood. The squealing calf had run right into Bill's long legs, looking desperately for protection.

"If you don't run this hateful big-nosed pest off the place, Bill, I will." Poor Velma was heaving and the rake was waving. "He's going to eat us all out of house and home." The four-legged menace hid squarely behind the tall woodchopper, rolling his little eyes and squirming his aching back up against his protector.

"Well, now, I reckon that's my fault. I was goin' t' put th' fence up around th' cabin, but I ain't got enough poles out yet. I'll start in tomorrow." Bill sat down on a block of wood. His prized pet gave him an affectionate nudge, and Bill narrowly missed slicing his hand on the double-bitted axe.

Velma, tired out and still exasperated, glared at the moose. "Well, I just hope the game warden catches up with you. Keeping that thing around here is against the law." She waved her rake. The calf ducked his head and pushed closer to Bill. "Now, *look*, this little devil can leave *anytime*. What th' law says is, no game animal can be kept in captivity." Bill waved his hands at the timbered mountain back of the log buildings. "He's free as the air."

"Well, they'll have to change the laws, then, or I will," said Velma, starting back to the house to get dinner. "That ornery little bog trotter has got *us* in captivity, and *I*, for one, am getting awfully blamed tired of it."

"Only time he ever *was* in captivity was the day the minister came," Bill called after her, "an' you're th' one let him out that time!"

That was a sore point with Velma. She slammed the door.

The Suitor

A few weeks after this, Velma's prim old maid sister came up for a visit. She was a retired county school superintendent and an active despot in her church. Minnie had an ill-disguised disapproval of Bill's way of life, so her visits were painful for him. This time Bill had a good excuse to get away for awhile. He had to drive the old pickup into town to get plumbing fixtures, as the indoor facilities had gone out of kilter.

The old gal used the very latest perfume, a heady mixture that attracted nobody but the pet moose, and he had a pungent odor all his own. This militant old sister detested the bog trotter, but Nosy was the only suitor she had ever had in a long life of pedagogical frustration. She rarely came to the ranch, mostly because of him and his delighted attentions. For this Bill was privately grateful. When she did show up, the moose was Johnny on the spot, if the wind was right. Her violent reactions didn't bother this gangly-legged suitor; on her visits he'd try to push open doors and bust windows. On one historic occasion he tried to cram into her car with her.

Ol' Minnie had just gone out to the Chic Sales when the assistant county assessor drove up to the house. He was a deacon in Minnie's church, and they had small charity for each other. His job took him over a lot of the county, and he had developed a newsy neighborliness. This habit made him welcome at lonely ranches and helped to soften the blow of more taxes. Velma and the assessor were in the kitchen talking over county happenings, when weird screams and delighted squeals brought them on the run to the back porch. The old school mom stood in the door of the rickety Chic Sales throwing heavy mail-order catalogs at her detested sloppy-nosed admirer. Her lurid invective was highly interesting, but her aim was poor. Evidently the affectionate willow-cruncher thought his beloved was only playing a game, for he was up close, snorting his happy approval. Poor Minnie was out of vocabulary and ammunition when her giggling sister and the interested assessor rescued her. Velma ran the young moose off with her broom, and the scoop-heavy deacon soon left on more official business.

The dictator of many a schoolroom, long skinny arms akimbo,

stood on the back porch staring in rage at the fast disappearing car. As the lodgepole pines hid the joyous reporter's bouncing vehicle, she whirled on her sister. Velma retreated into the kitchen and stood at the table rolling out pie dough. She expected Bill home ·for dinner, and this was a bang-up meal she was fixing up in honor of Minnie's visit.

The irate old maid stood glowering at her sister. Velma was choking down mirth as she lined her pie tins with dough. "Never in my born days has anything so embarrassed me, or have I been subjected to such insulting indignities." Minnie's bejewelled horn-rimmed glasses trembled on her long intellectual nose. "Between that misbegotten, moth-eaten, malicious moose pet of that mule-headed husband of yours, and that hypocritical, tongue-wagging church mouse of a cheap politician," she paused for a righteous breath, "I'll be the laughing stock of the whole stupid county!" Her long pendant earrings jangled in tune with her vibrating jaws, as Velma shoved the pies in the oven, and put more wood in the shining stove.

Nosy in the meantime took his disappointed majesty back around the barn. He spied his arch-enemy, the tiger-striped tabby cat, stalking a mouse. The frustrated yearling sensed honor regained and took after Tabby. The cat whipped around the log barn, hell for breakfast, with the humpy calf in close pursuit. After losing the chase to the hay shed, Nosy was shoving his long snoot up against a bale of hay, wondering where in Hades she'd got to. He found out in a hurry, for the cat's kittens were in a warm pocket under that bale. She had no catalogs to throw, but she thought maybe moose eat kittens. So she came out of her chute with a snarling yowl, lit on Nosy's high withers, sank her sets of sharp spurs in his humpy shoulders, and went to scratching, Cheyenne style, rowdy dow.

This moose didn't buck but he sure did bawl. And then he suddenly decided misery loves company. The tigerish contestant was making a buzz-saw ride on the lonesome calf, but left her mount and jumped up on the porch roof when the frantic pet burst up against the screen door to the kitchen.

Bill was just coming in the front door of the cabin with his arms full of store plunder when he was knocked down and run over by his terrified, high-heeled sister-in-law. He got up in a bruised hurry when he heard the screaming hullaballoo at the back door. Running around the cabin, Bill was just in time to get a second and third dose of moositis, for he was knocked down and run over by the fleeing calf

38

The contestant was making a buzz-saw ride.

He was knocked down and run over by the calf and Velma in turn.

and Velma in turn. She had her broom working, and her flow of language showed that education ran in her family. Breathless, his wife helped poor down-trodden Bill to his unsteady feet. He could hardly stand. The tough old hillbilly had moose and woman tracks all over his aching carcass. Velma suddenly thought of Minnie when she heard a muffled screech. A heavy door slammed, and down the road went her sister's new car. Right behind it, his long nose high in the air, was the calf moose. He was in an ungainly trot, but making good time.

After he had heard the story of Nosy's last exploits, Bill agreed that the youngster would have to find a new home. "When he shows up again, I'll run him off." Bill privately hoped, though, if Nosey did show up it would be when Minnie paid them another visit. That would help some.

Nosy and the Pin-Ups

Ol' Bill started to swear when the worn pipe wrench slipped again, then he remembered the company Velma was entertaining in the front room. He could hear the voice of Hector McBain, a deacon in Velma's church.

"Ol' Fact 'n' Figgers tryin' t'sell Vel some more insurance," Bill blew on his skinned-up knuckles. He just got a fresh holt with the wrench when he heard hoarse whispering back of him.

"Say, Bill, I know your facilities are not in order now." Old McBain was leaning over the bowlegged plumber and looking furtively over his shoulder towards the teacups rattling in the next room. "But I need to go, and do you have a place?"

Thompson wearily got up from the jumble of pipe fittings on the floor and pointed out the window. "See that building right next ta the bunkhouse? That's what we're usin' till I git this layout goin' again."

The portly man pursed his lips, then started out the back door at a half trot. Thompson saw McBain go in the Chic Sales, and then he sat down on the floor again to tinker with the assortment of pipe fittings.

The hornets figured that their nest was anchored plenty strong under the eaves above the door of the shaky building. They got kind of waspy when their home was half shook loose as the deacon slammed the door. When those angry bugs in the yellow jackets started to swarm through the many cracks in the building, the distracted insurance man was stung to violent action. He kicked a couple of shaky boards loose in the back of the trembling edifice, squeezed through, and galloped off in the direction of his car, parked in front of Thompson's cabin. Moocher, from under the back porch, saw the frantic man in a high lope, slapping at his head with one hand and holding his britches with the other. He helped speed the frustrated deacon on his way.

Life seemed sort of uncertain lately for the moose. He sensed an unfriendly atmosphere around the ranch. He had sneaked out of the timber and was now chewing his cud behind the barn. When he heard Moocher's enthusiastic barking over by the bunkhouse, Nosy heaved

The peppery and astonished face of Mrs. Hector McBain.

up on his hind legs to investigate the proceedings.

The moose calf happened to see the loose boards lying on the ground behind the sittin' and thinkin' establishment, so he walked up to see about the new opening in the back of the building. The hornets by this time had given up and buzzed away elsewhere to discuss a new location for their headquarters. Having become quite a student of human nature, the nosy calf stuck his long head and short neck through the deacon's door. He got to studying the pin-up pictures that Tony Belknap had nailed to the inside of the old door last fall.

Lulu McBain got uneasy over the long absence of her crusty old husband. Finding where he'd gone, she called several times. Old Heck didn't answer, so Lulu got alarmed, ran up to the small and silent building, and jerked the door open.

The moose hadn't yet come to any nearsighted conclusions on the lithographed dreams of Tony the cowboy. He was now patiently chewing his cud, still staring at the pictures. His attention was rudely diverted from a pretty pin-up to the peppery and astonished face of Mrs. Hector McBain.

Belknap was having his jug ears lifted in Harry Clipper's barber shop when he heard the story. "Yuh don't believe it, huh? Why, you birds don't know the half of it. You'd be surprised at whut ol' Bill teaches that dang moose. Sure he uses th' Chic Sales. Why, that nutty packer regards th' blasted thing as a member o' the family. Wouldn't supprise me none if they feed 'im at th' table next!"

Just Married

"My gosh, Jeannie, we forgot to bring a lantern." Colvin Larsen put another small branch on the campfire. "I just looked through all our things, and no candles or flashlights, either." Jeannie, the young bride of a few hours, sat on a log close by her young husband. "M-m-m, Colvin, I like it dark."

Nosy, on his way home from visiting some upland swamps, was coming down a trail when he smelled the smoke. Over in a small timber-surrounded park he saw the dim shape of a car lit up by flickering firelight. The sounds and smells coming from the two vague shapes sitting close together on a log aroused Nosy's sense of conquest. Maybe this *was* a closed corporation, but the dark night and his ever-present appetite decided the moose to look over the prospectus. The honeymooners were reaching into a well-filled basket and feeding each other tidbits. The dying embers of the small fire didn't give much light, but the two young lovers, engrossed in their new status, didn't need any.

About the time Jeannie reached into the basket for another cookie, the infernal triangle thrust its long nose in between the happy affairs of the newlyweds. As the happy bride handed a nice mayonnaise concoction up to Colvin, Nosy daintily took the offering and started chewing it with gusto.

Jeannie said, "Oh, Colvin, dear, isn't this a dream, just like we planned!" Nosy, busy chewing a pickle, gave a little simpering whine. Colvin, not to be outdone by Jeannie's generosity, answered, "Here's a real nice olive and lettuce deal, honey." As the bog trotter very delicately received the choice tidbit, Colvin didn't want to look. He thought, "Jeannie sure does make a lot of noise eating." His beloved, reaching down for another morsel, was really put out. "My, Colvin is sure a sloppy eater. Funny I never noticed it before." Oddly enough, both the newlyweds were feeding themselves, too, besides supposedly feeding each other. With the new development, the erstwhile happy couple couldn't bear to look at one another.

It occurred to them both that "this must have been a strenuous day, the way we're disposing of this food." As they blindly handed up food to the new member of the troupe, the moocher, not wanting to

Nosy, busy chewing a pickle gave a little simpering whine.

show favorites with such generous new-found friends, rested his chin alternately on each shoulder, and entered into the slowed-down conversation with gulpy gargles. As the chompy smacking continued, both Colvin and his wife were privately thinking of all they'd heard and read of what it takes to make a solid, long-lasting marriage. "Smackey smack. Chompety chomp." "This fifty-fifty business of give and take." This business of such gusty and vociferous appreciation of food would be hard to take for a lifetime. "Oh, my," she thought. "This is terrible," he shuddered. As they fed themselves, and, unknowing, their guest, the disillusioned couple kept their gaze averted. The three-way disposal of food continued.

The distracted young lovers suddenly became aware of a new crisis. The wind rose slightly, just as Nosy nestled closer, in breathless ecstacy, to these fine providers. They wondered simultaneously how in the world so delicate a subject as halitosis should come to their minds. As this fresh danger to a continued happy marriage showed up, the random thoughts became intense. "It's a touchy situation" . . . "What friends could I ask to approach the subject?" . . . . . "These short engagements, hmmm" . . . . . "Never woulda' thought it could be *so terribly awful!*"

The unhappy couple, busy worrying about this noisy and smelly flaw in their early wedded bliss, let the campfire die down. Their attention wasn't on food. In the dark their selection became hit and miss. Jeannie handed up a pickled pepper, which found its spicy way into the bogtrotter's busy jaws. The resulting wheezy expectoration suddenly blew up the coals and put a different light on the situation.

At the first strangling wheeze, thinking to put their arms around each other in alarmed protection, the pair found themselves hugging the hairy moose. The sadly reproachful stare of Nosy's little pig eyes didn't soften the screamy yells as the honeymooners climbed two separate and surprised trees.

During the flurry of his sudden abandonment, Nosy found that he had stepped on a hot coal and now had a burned place on the underside of a front toe. Seeking solace and help from his friends in the upper brackets, he wore a path between the trees. His mournful come-help-me squealed whines made the separated lovebugs sure a bear had joined the joyful procession, and the darkness helped the illusion. The anxious queries of the divorced providers were rudely interrupted by the floppy-nosed member of the triangle. He would limp back and forth from tree to tree, and at every desperate attempt at communication would belch his whiny complaints.

47

The bridal suite had branched out into two barky roosts through no previous plans of the besieged couple. "If this is togetherness," the pet mused bitterly in his boggy mind, "I'll put in with yuh. Home was never like this." Jeannie and Colvin entertained similar thoughts. For them it was lucky the night was warm, as their clothes weren't the class for that type of high living. Being young, they didn't suffer much. This bridal couple was different from the general run. It wasn't darkness they craved, it was light, that would identify the unknown menace at the foot of their trees.

It seemed like eternity to the people up above. But it was only a couple of hours before one of the coals from the scattered campfire decided to help them out. A slight breeze whipped the coal into igniting some vagrant and very dry branches under their perches. When the blaze flared up, the cold couple saw a small moose rise up from their wedding gift blankets behind the log. Colvin recognized Nosy from a former visit to Bill's ranch. He scrambled down out of his tree with a relieved yell. He got hold of a dead limb and whacked the moose across the nose a few times. Nosy took off in a scared hurry and disappeared into the heavy timber.

The two new Larsens soon had a big fire going. By the time they had their tent pitched they were able to laugh at the only moose shivaree they'd ever heard of.

The rest of the night was very peaceful.

The next morning after a late breakfast they decided to move camp to a small lake just off the forest road. They'd packed everything into the car before Colvin discovered the ignition key had been left on.

"Well, darn it, Jeannie, looks like I'll have to go down to Thompson's ranch." Colvin kicked at a tire. "Maybe I can get Ol' Bill to come up in his pickup and give us a pull. There's enough juice for ignition if we can just start her." The bride sat on a log and stared at her husband, then she started to giggle. Colvin got mad for the first time in his young married life. When she kept on laughing, he started to splutter. Then the thought struck him that she had been too long up in the air, and might be just a trifle touched.

"Oh, honey, with all those cuts and scratches you got going up the tree last night, you wouldn't dare." The bridegroom had his jaw dropped down on his brisket now as he looked his new wife over. She had a cut over one pretty eyebrow and some scratches across her throat and chin. Otherwise she looked the loveliest bride he ever saw. Larsen looked at the old model car, then back at Jeannie. "Are you *sure* you feel all right, Sweetie-pie? Why shouldn't I dare?"

48

Jeannie giggled when she pointed to all the soapwritings their friends had plastered on the car. "That's why, you big ninny." Colvin had a small garage in town. Lots of people thought he was the best mechanic in Roaring River. Some said he had only wheels in his head. But when he saw "Just Married" printed on the back window a great light dawned. He had to sit down beside Jeannie and laugh, too.

Finally he jacked the hind wheels up in the air and cranked his engine by turning a wheel in gear. The motor caught. Soon they were chugging up the road. As they passed an opening in the timber they could look down on Bill Thompson's ranch cabins in the valley. Just below the corrals they caught a glimpse of Nosy, on the edge of a willow bog. He was looking at their moving car with a moldy stare. The couple waved at the moose and drove laughing up the road.

Picnic

A row of shiny cars was lined up over in the shade of pines on the far side of a big park. Not far off, a laughing crowd of brightly dressed people were clustered around some fishermen, who were showing off their fine catches of trout. A few children were trying to climb trees, playing tag, and skylarking around in the tall yellow grass.

The meeting of the Federation of Fair Play to Nature was a great success. Some of the big city members were there, and the Grand High Potentate of all the national clubs had given a speech. The picnic following it was to be held in Moose Park—"Oh, sure, a lot of us have fished up there." The Boy Scout leader knew the country. He said, "Well, it's a big meadow surrounded by timber. Creek runs through the edge of it. We'll have a good time. Safe for the kids." A member of the local ski club said, "We go up to the Pass to ski, go right by the park. Never saw a moose there. Not many left. Named Moose Park by early settlers. What moose there's left are probably higher in the mountains this time of year. Only takes a couple hours to drive. Good road."

Maybe clothes don't make the moose, but Nosy didn't know the difference. He'd had a bath, in his private wallow a couple miles above Ol' Bill's ranch. After he'd scrambled out of his cozy mud hole, he gulped a few snorts of the delicious brown liquid that floated on the surface of the pool nearby—this thick liquor of spring water and years of rotted willow leaves, swamp grass, and deceased frogs makes moose act the way they do. So the young bull, strutting out of his spruce shaded bar, felt like he was able to face the world again. As the swamp angel walked over to the edge of the mountain park, he heard sounds over by the creek. Surveying the scene from behind a tree, he saw some women spreading blankets and white cloths on the ground, and scurrying back and forth from automobiles on the far side of the grassy park.

Those jolts of willow liquor from his private stock were just getting hold of Bill's pet. He flapped his big ears and rolled his eyes to get control of himself. The moose felt that the brave deserve the fair, and the small breeze told him that there might be a fairly edible meal for a young moose bound to get ahead. So he backed up into the heavy timber to take a sashay around for a more strategic assault. Things had started to look up on Roaring River. The closer he got to the line of cars, the surer his sensitive snoot was that prosperity was just around the bend. But his dreams of sudden subsidy were shattered by the kid up a tree.

A small girl standing on the ground was applauding the brave efforts of an older boy. He was perched eight feet or so up a tree, poking a stick at a chattering pine squirrel in the top. The girl caught a glimpse of Nosy moving close by, suddenly screamed, "Bear! Bear!" and took off at a yelping run for her mother over by the parked cars. The bog trotter's plan for collecting tribute for the invasion of his mountains was deferred for awhile. Irritated by all the yelpy screams, he was forced to make a wider detour.

The big game hunter was so startled by the scream, "Bear!" and by the noisy desertion of his ally, that he lost all holts and busted down through the branches to the ground. He lit on his eight-year-old rump, breaking the jar with his brace of quick draw six-shooters; and he had twice the lung power of any four little girls.

Galloping across the meadow, yelling, "Timmee, oh Timmee," came a big lady in pink shorts. She was waving a pan in one hand and a big long-handled spoon in the other. Several of the crowd running behind her skidded in the trail of purple pudding, but soon most of the local chapter were grouped around Timmy and his breathless Mommy. She had her arms clamped around him, and was yelling, "Get a doctor, oh, get a doctor, why doncha, somebody!"

When the small actor on the ground saw all the attention his audience was giving him, he squirmed out of his mother's arms and wailed, "I run 'em off, they was after Suzie." He pointed with his one good six-shooter, "They went that-a-way. Three big bears." While the women were collecting the kids, the men were ka-whacking tree trunks with dead limbs, throwing rocks, and shouting into the dark timber, careful not to go farther into the mysterious jungle.

In the meantime, on the far side of the grassy park, the young moose, closing in on the line of deserted cars, found several with open doors. Before the women got back to the autos to start assembling food for the hungry gang, the long-nosed investigator was suddenly given more time to evaluate the hidden assets. Their fears subsiding, the chattering women were coming back to the base of supplies, casually followed by the men, when they were electrified by some new screams down by the creek. "Wah, wa-a-a-, ouee!" A strong snag had a fat boy firmly by a hip pocket. "Oh, Dadee, help me-e-!" He was kicking and flailing his arms. One chubby hand bristled with quills. "Oh, Dad-dee, the cactus kitty hit me with his tail!" Three or four men ran to stand underneath the tree. "Hold on, sonny, hold on." — "Hope that pocket holds." — "Man, look at that paw." The pine needles and twigs showered down into their eyes.

While the experts on the ground shouted advice, the plump youngster, full of tears and quills, was lowered to his hysterical mother. . . . "Hey, there's Johnnie Brown up there." All the eyes had been on the porcupine, and now they saw the lad higher up. He was staring down at the quill pig just below him. Frozen with terror, he was draped around the rough bark, and couldn't make a sound. The defendant in the case wasn't lifting a quill. He was out on a limb and knew it. "That murderous porcupine" was soon dislodged and now lay null and void on the ground.

The high-climbing explorer in the treetop had an athletic father who was also the executioner. He couldn't sweet-talk his boy down out of the tree, so he was soon in a bear-hugging climb up the rough ladder. The long-nosed collector of internal revenue was lucky. All the rushing back and forth of his clients had given him time to sample some of the best products of several chain stores. He found an especially appetizing bowl of salad on the back seat of a new station wagon. Both doors were conveniently left open. As he braced his long hind legs on the ground, he was comfortably resting his folded front legs on the luxurious carpet of the car floor. While daintily discarding unwanted portions over the seat, he could watch the actions of his patrons through the hospitably open door on the opposite side. He was having a snuffling good time when he heard some shouts of laughter mixed with muffled ungenteel curses.

What intrigued the young moose and delighted the sympathetic crowd gathered around, was what happened when the exasperated father deposited his son on the ground. His new high-heeled boots slipped on the slick pine needles, and he slid down the grassy slope right on top of the recently deceased. When he was helped up, he knew that there was some sticky fine print in poor Porky's last will and testament. The angry man had gathered more souvenirs with his aching differential. When the climber had started up the tree he was hungry, but now he was the only one in the bunch whose mind wasn't on food.

When the mayor's wife wasn't playing bridge, she was organizing new plays, with the lead somehow or other usually falling to her own modest self. This time she had missed a lot of dramatic potentials, for she had lost or misplaced her hearing aid. While the tree climbing rescue expedition had taken place, she was gathering spruce and pine cones for bridge favors. When she had an armful she went back to her station wagon. Just as the near-sighted lady came around a small green tree close to her car, her glasses lost their grip on her patrician nose, and fell dangling at the end of the golden chain attached to her ample bosom.

Nosy was still in the same position. He was comfortable, and the sights and cuisine suited him. But when the plump lady came up behind him things happened fast. Mistaking Nosy's jaunty gray-clad rear quarters for her husband stooping over to get cigars out of the glove compartment, the lady playfully cried, "Boo!" and dropped her load of pine cones close to his hind feet.

Thinking that Velma Thompson was on the job, the young boarder dived out the open door in a conscience stricken hurry. When his front feet hit the ground, his hind feet struck the big brass salad bowl. That leverage helped the fleeing moose escape, but the heavy bowl was shot backwards onto Mrs. Jones's twenty dollar permanent. While she lay screaming on her back, clawing ten thousand islands of dressing out of her just built silvery locks, Nosy was trotting right through the tempting feast spread around on the grassy meadow. The shrieking and screaming of the arrangement committee, as they crawled and fell away from the flap-eared pet's frontal retreat, reminded Nosy of sounds he had grown used to from more youthful days, only louder.

The mountain meadow calmed down now. The people gathered round, ready to partake of most of the delayed picnic. Everybody quieted down, waiting for the blessing. One member looked around: "Say, folks, our Grand High Potentate is missing. The last I seen of him, he was fishing, just down the creek. We'd better look him up. He's to ask the blessing. Let's just hold up a minute. I'll go get him."

The highest officer of the federation had been asked to visit this local chapter and attend their annual picnic. He was a philanthropist and very conservative. Besides being highly respected, he was an avid fisherman. While several men went down to the creek bordering the park to locate the missing man, the disgruntled calf moose was back in his private bar. After a few quaffs of the Fountain of Moose, his swampy confidence was restored. He was soon headed back toward the picnic.

The searchers didn't have far to go. Moose Park wasn't misnamed; it was in the middle of the local concentration of the long-nosed animals. But no such thought entered the head of the Potentate as he

53

stooped to go through the heavy growth of willows below the big pool. He'd caught some nice brook trout and thought he'd make a last try before he went back to the gathering. His fishing hat, full of hand-tied flies and spare hooks, fell down over his sweaty forehead, as he lowered his rod tip to squirm through the ropy growths. The natural doorway he crawled through turned out to be the hind legs of a huge bull moose and cut short his ambition for one last brookie.

This bull was sampling some of the delicious tips of the luxuriant willow growths and was at peace with the world. When his tender belly was suddenly pricked by a hand-honed Royal Coachman, he felt that his privacy was invaded, so he left the dining room in high-geared dudgeon. The noise the moose made couldn't hold a candle to the one the Potentate made. He was a solid business man and was used to being on top, even if he was a small sort of Napoleon. One of the members later named this particular spot the Exodus Pool; that is, after they extracted the disarranged fisherman from the water he was drowning in.

The kids had waited long enough, so to restrain them, their mammas had sneaked stray bits of sandwiches and had done a little undercover nibbling themselves. Even the disgruntled heir of Porky's last quill and testament had regained some of his hunger. A dentist member of the group, with emergency instruments and snickering helpers, had relieved the beneficiary of most of the fine print from his anatomy.

Now everything was under control, and everybody was waiting. The Federation President was about to come out of his car, where he had gone for surface repairs and to change clothes. The high mogul was in the midst of hurriedly completing the overhaul, when he thought of something to give him more profound inspiration. He just ducked his head behind the back seat when his secret ritual was rudely interrupted. Nosy, casing the various rubber-tired joints, had come across the fanciest yet. And a window was open.

Just as the hammer-headed epicurean stuck his snout into the window, he stepped on the wreckage of an English-built fly rod lying on the ground. An expensive bamboo sliver gleefully inserted itself between two of the grafter's toes and jabbed with devilish abandon. Young Nosy gave an ouchy squeal right in the worshipping man's face, then wheeled around to disappear into the safer timber.

The hungrily waiting members of the Federation were astounded to see their barefooted Grand Potentate burst from his station wagon and run toward them. His shirt tail flapped against his colorful shorts, and he had a deathlike grip on a flat bottle halfway out of a fancy leather

Nosy gave an ouchy squeal.

case. The sounds he made indicated to the appreciative picnickers that here was no blessing; but that this Napoleon did have mule-driving ancestors.

The Bell

The only church the cowboy had ever attended was the Big One where he had spent his life. Now the canyon walls below Cathedral Cliffs re-echoed the sweet tones before the rider on the roan horse believed his ears.

"I'd know th' sound o' that bell anywhere. It's got a high ringin' sound like th' ol' mission bell down in town. Them chimes has gotta be on that Spook horse. Jest gotta be." Tony ran his big horse into the dark jungle of deadfalls, trying to make a circle above the musical sounds in the timber higher up. "Every time I hear his bell and take to him, he heads for the tall timber, an' I ain't seen him yet." Belknap had been hunting the bunch-quitter off and on for a week, and now figured he had the spooky pony dead to rights. The horse had strayed away from the cow-camp cavvy, and Tony needed him. Holding cattle on the mountain was rough work. His other ponies were overworked and this lone feeder had hid out from the job.

Ducking low limbs and jumping down timber, the horse hunters were making good time. From the sound of the noisy horse bell, Tony figured they were about to close in and nab the shirking renegade. The strawberry roan had the same ambition, but his smeller told him that *this* bell wasn't on any relative he'd ever claim. The cowboy spurred his horse over a huge deadfall. Roany hadn't heard about fools and angels, but he knew which was on his back when he high-centered on a snaggy tree trunk.

"By gorry, I've hunted Ol' Spook fer a week an' I'll be dad-burned if he's goin' ta git away this time!" The cowhand jabbed his hooks into the struggling horse. Tony's weight and his own 1000 pounds didn't tickle the roan's suffering briskit, so at the next jab the outraged horse whipped his head around and grabbed a mouthful of Tony's gittin'-on leg, just above his boot top. With an anguished howl, the horse-hunter fell out of his saddle and lit in a bramble of tree limbs.

The next morning Belknap was barely able to hobble out of the cow camp cabin. He'd spent half the night soaking his chewed-up leg in salt water. "I sure made uh poor trade," Tony mumbled. "Uh horse bite fer uh horse bell ain't what I had in mind."

57

The crippled-up cowboy had piled up limbs and green branches on both sides of Roany's teeter-totter until the horse had enough footing to scramble off the dead tree. "Ol' Roany didn't need no lawyer, I'll say that fer him. It was a clear case o' self defense. But why'n hell did he hafta wear out th' cinch on that tree he was perched on?" Tony felt of the bruised rump on his off side. When the cowboy had mounted Roany for the painful ride back to cow camp, the horse walked a few steps and the saddle fell off; the old cinch had parted. The horse hunter had a crippled left leg and a sore right hip to sort of make a balanced ride. "By gorry, it ain't ridin' that makes a hand bowlegged, it's th' things that happen when ye're jest a-trying to."

Tony thought awhile and groaned to himself, "I think I'll quit this here cow-punchin' before my carcass gits bent up too late ta weld. Mebbe I kin git me a job washin' dishes, my arms're long enough so's I won't drownd."

A few days hard riding kept Tony's mind off his sore leg. It was healing and showing no sign of infection. He found a bunch of his cows and calves down on the wrong side of the divide and threw them back on their own range. Things looked pretty good now, outside of the strayed horse he hadn't caught up with.

One warm sunny morning Tony decided to clean up the cabin and wash all his clothes and blankets. He had a couple of five-gallon tins of water heating on the cabin stove and was washing out the last of the job back of the cabin. The old tub and the piece of corrugated roofing tin nailed on a board did the job good enough for Tony. The store-bought scrubbing board had come up missing last hunting season, so Tony had a new machine. The clothesline, from a tree down by the creek up to a cabin end log, was hung full of blankets and most of Tony's forty years gatherings. The cowboy was feeling pretty good to have this job about over. He had on an old ragged hat, his oldest undershirt, and a wornout pair of Levis on his skinny carcass. He was playing a tune on the tin roofing with his best shirt and was soapsuds from his wet boots clear up to his knobby elbows.

He was wringing out his polka dot prize when he heard, "Sure is a good washday, Tony." Startled, he bumped the old washtub off the stump, slipped on the fallen soap, and sat down on the wet ground. A wrangler friend of his and a row of laughing dudes sat their horses just beyond the cabin.

Tony'd eaten his dinner and was down to the corral saddling up a horse when he heard some of the dudes talking to their guide as they were fitting their fly rods together, down on the creek.

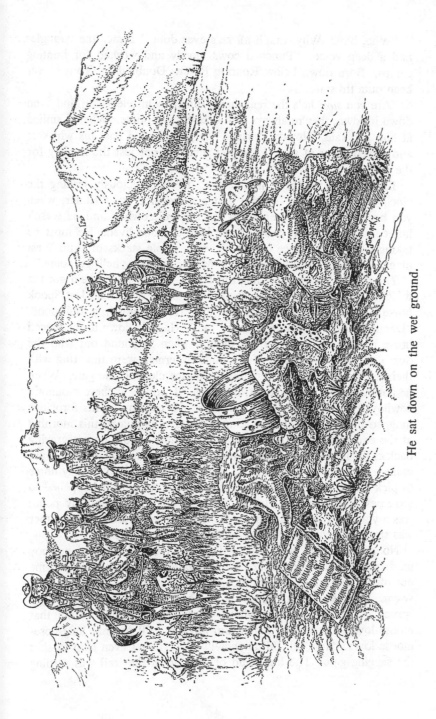

He sat down on the wet ground.

"Who, him? Why, that'll all he's ever done," Elmer the wrangler had a deep voice. "Punched cows mostly and worked for hunting camps. Born down below Roaring River. Doubt if ol' Tony's ever been outa th' state."

"Are you *sure* he's the real thing, Elmer? On television, and even down in town, they're always well dressed and polite. When I smiled at him and said, 'Howdy, partner,' he just grunted past his whiskers and waved a bar of soap. Are you sure he's not just the flunkey for the *real* cowboy?"

Tony gritted his teeth at that one. He was viciously jerking the cinch tighter when he heard a young voice pipe up. "Elmer, when you brought me up yesterday to meet a *real* cowboy and he wasn't home, I peeked in his cabin to see how this one lived. He must be taking a correspondence course. There's whole stacks of Wild West magazines piled close to his bunk. Maybe someday he'll graduate."

The day had started out fine for Tony. He felt lucky, he'd got the washing all done, and he was determined to run down that lost Spook horse if it was the last thing he ever did. He was now in a foul mood. "Damn dudes, they're dumb, damn 'em." He rode down to the fenced horse pasture to catch a fresh mount, when he found out who the dumb one was. A couple of the dude fishermen were tinkering with their fishing rods behind a clump of spruce close to the gate. When he got off his horse to open it, he heard, "I wonder if these mountain cowboys ride moose." They didn't see the cowboy or his ferocious mug, so the voice went on talking. "I was riding along this morning at the end of the bunch when I noticed those saddle horses grazing back of the fence. Two of them had bells tied around their necks. Sure make a loud noise. Then when I dropped my pipe I got off my horse to pick it up. As I was about to step back up on him, I happened to look past a long neck of trees. There, feeding in a small lily pond, was a young moose. He had *two* bells, one was natural and the other was strapped around his neck. Sure make a loud noise."

No grizzly could have equalled the sounds the enraged cowboy made when he nearly wrecked the old gate open. When Tony came out of the pasture on a high lope, his fresh mount was already in a sweat. The two scared fishermen perched high in the same snaggy spruce heard "the crazy cowboy" yowling to himself, "Damn that moose-lovin' Thompson, damn him anyhow. I'll fix that long-nose-moose lover, damn Ol' Bill anyhow!" Tony didn't even stop to shut the sagging gate. The big cloud of dust down the trail was settling before the uneasy fishermen climbed down to look for their thrown away fly rods.

By the time Tony had ridden the steep six miles down the mountain trail to "Moose-lovin' Thompson's" ranch, his leg was giving him what for, and his mind was set on "turnin' ol' Bill every way but loose," if he could catch that ol' pet-makin' Bill where he could get at him.

As he rode down off Bull Ridge he got a good glimpse of Bill's place. There was Velma working in her backyard among her delphiniums. Tony caught sight of Bill peeling some poles down by the barn corrals, so he rode around out of sight of the cabin, figuring on having it out with Ol' Bill without any rolling pin interference.

Just as he rode up to the corral, all hot and bothered, Bill looked up. "Well, by hell, Tony Belknap, jest in time for coffee. Yuh look like yuh need it. Down in the mouth and all lathered up." Tony got stiffly off his horse. He was about to tell Bill off when Nosy the pet moose came around the barn. He took one look at Tony and his mane came up. He started to stomp his front feet as he came toward the astonished man. He had only one bell and it was his own hair-covered one. While the crestfallen warrior watched, Ol' Bill picked up a stick and run Nosy off.

As the hostile moose disappeared around the barn, Tony sat down on a pile of corral poles and wearily pulled out his tobacco sack to roll a smoke. The cowboy felt that he was a fool twisted by knaves to make a trap for moose, but he didn't dare admit it.

"By hell, Bill, them danged Bar Zee dudes's got the cow camp surrounded. I thought I'd come down t'associate with humans while them dern city slickers fish th' creek out. Besides, I aimed t'go t'the ranch ta tell the boss I'm outa salt fer th' cows."

While Bill and Tony walked up to the house for coffee, Ol' Bill noticed the limp Tony couldn't control. "Jest hit a low limb while I was ridin' through some timber, tryin' t'bend back some cows," was the quickest lie Tony could think of. He was sure that if he let the true story out, he'd be christened "The Hungry Horse Kid" from then on.

By evening the disillusioned cowboy was down at the home ranch. The boss said he'd pack some stock salt up to the cow camp in a day or two. After supper and a good sleep in the bunkhouse the cowboy felt better. He ate breakfast, and felt strong enough for the ride back to the cow camp.

"By hell, Tony, you shoulda been here a week or so ago." The boss

61

was laughing at the joke he'd played. "Bill Thompson's pet moose showed up here, and he got t' jumpin' over inta a new stack yard full of hay, 'n' foolin' around th' barn. I thought I'd play a good one on Ol' Bill, he's so proud o' th' dang thing. I roped th' dang grafter, tied 'im down, an' strapped a bell around his neck. You'da laughed yer head off when I turned 'im loose. He took off in a clangin' hurry, stampeded th' milk cows when he piled over th' new buck fence we built this spring. Th' last I seen 'im, he was jangle-bongin' through th' heavy timber, straight up Bull Ridge. You cud hear 'im a long time."

Tony stared at the boss. "Say, now, when we hazed th' cows up th' mountain this spring, I took *all* the bells off'n the ranch fer my horse string. Where didja git hold of th' bell?"

"By hell, Tony, I fergot t'tell yuh." The boss grinned. "That horse Spook showed up here about ten days ago. That's his bell I put on Bill's moose."

The cowboy thought of Nosy staying home and minding his own business, so he didn't tell the boss he'd wasted a bell on a wild moose. Tony rode off up the trail mumbling to himself, "Mebbe I'd better wait before I git me a job a-washin' dishes. By gorry, I kin still hear good, even if I ain't yet graduated."

Travois

While she was sorting out her freshly washed clothes, Velma happened to look out a kitchen window and saw Bill crawl out from under his decrepit old pickup. When he sat down on the running board of the "Old Maid," as they called the eccentric truck, Velma went out to hear the verdict. Bill sat with his head in his hands. "I guess I'll hafta give up, Velma. We c'n git ta town with th' old girl, but I'm afraid she's on 'er last legs." Bill stopped talking to rub the butting head of Nosy, who had come up to get in on the deal. "Near's I c'n figger she's got th' gallopin' consumption. Her rings has outwore her engagement. The Old Maid's gotta go. We'll hafta deal for a better one."

Moocher, behind Velma, growled at Nosy.

Remembering other deals, and how trusting and gullible Bill was, Vel started off with, "We've got to watch our step, Bill. Some car dealers are like some lawyers seem to be." Bill reached into a pocket for his mouth harp, to tantalize Nosy with. He played a high-pitched whiny tune. He and Velma both laughed to watch the moose calf in a stiff-legged trot, squealing and bunting at the pickup's crumpled fenders. Old Moocher, the dog, sat off to one side howling and yelping at the sky.

"What's lawyers got t'do with car dealers anyhow?" Bill, out of wind, got tired of watching Nosy's and Moocher's gyrations, and was hammering out the harp's moisture on his knee. He just grunted when Velma replied, "Lots of car dealers are like lots of lawyers, they're masters of subterfuge and evasion."

"Look, Vel, you're thinkin' o'Nosy. He *likes* my music. He just *pretends* he don't."

Velma stared at Bill and Nosy in exasperation. "I give up. Well, I've got to iron a dress and get ready. It'll take me about an hour. Then we can go to town to see about another pickup."

Bill got up off the running board and started towards his shop. "I'll git some tools and stuff. I might as well fix that corner of roofing on the back porch while you're a-gittin' ready."

Her irons were hot—been heating up all morning on the wood stove. Having tested one with a wet finger, Velma was busy ironing a towngoing dress in time with her record player. Out a window she saw Nosy scratching his rump on a fender of the forlorn pickup. Remembering the show he'd put on for Bill's mouth harp, Vel stopped ironing for a minute to put "The Irish Washerwoman" on the record player. She opened up a window, turned the volume up high, and giggled at the antics of the long-legged bog-trotter. He was trotting around the pickup, squealing and grunting in frustration. Every once in a while he'd stop and bunt at the truck. Finally he went out of sight at a fast, humpy trot.

Velma had the volume turned up so high she didn't hear the yelling hullabaloo around the corner of the back porch. She resumed ironing, and was dreamily listening to one of her hifalutin (Bill called it) college records, when she heard hoarse mumbling as somebody fumbled at the screen door on the back porch.

When Velma saw the black and bloody streaked figure in tattered clothes stagger toward her, she instantly thought of the morning's radio report of a crazy man on the loose. She grabbed up Bill's big game rifle off his gun rack, hurriedly threw a live shell into the chamber, and was aiming wildly at the dripping apparition in the doorway when she realized it was her Bill, in a crude and painful disguise.

Vel doctored up Bill's cuts and scratches. He insisted she use his special sulpha-bear's-grease salve on his skinned-up face and knees. She didn't know whether to laugh or cry at the moose-maimed old hillbilly. So she did both.

"I was standing halfway up on that ladder," Bill muttered through his puffy lips. "I had just tacked down that last piece of roofin' and was pourin' tar when it happened." Bill, leaning over, had his head over a washtub. Velma was gingerly picking roofing tacks out of his sticky toupee.

Just a week ago Ol' Bill had undergone one of the town barber's grizzly bear crew cuts, for which he was now grateful. His smiling housewife was using turpentine to get the tar out of his hair, and Bill just knew the hair would come out. "Gittin' thin up there, anyhow," he muttered to himself. When he had to stand up suddenly to straighten out the kink in his neck, some of the turpentine dripped down his back a little too far. Bill dern lear lost his temper when Vel fell over into a chair in a giggling fit as Ol' Bill danced around howling and holding his backsides, his tattered and water-soaked overalls and shirt fluttering in his war dance.

Finally the dilapidated guide was some calmer. He was peacefully drinking coffee and eating some of his wife's delicious pie.

64

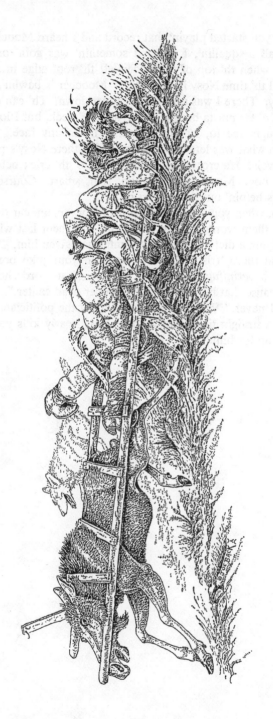

Nosy's pretty good with a travois.

"When you started playin' that record and I heard Moocher barkin' and th' calf a-squallin', I figgered somethin' was goin' on. I *knew* there was when th' top of th' ladder left th' roof edge in a hell of a hurry. All th' time Nosy is squallin' 'n' Moocher is bawlin', but I was kinda busy. There I was a-ridin' th' ladder down. Th' can o' tacks 'n' th' bucket o' tar musta been travelin' neck 'n' neck, but I lost th' race. What brought me to, was ol' Moocher lickin' my face. I was still a-layin' on what was left o' th' ladder. That there Nosy's pretty good with a travois. He crossed th' deepest part o' th' crick before he lost me in th' bog. Musta been travelin' right smart. Course Moocher probly was helpin' out the percession.

"Velma, when you was mixin' up them lawyers an' car dealers, you musta got them words twisted." Ol' Bill had spent last winter's evenings studying a dictionary a dude hunter had given him. "When you played that there 'Irish Washerwoman' on your juke box it musta acted like a *vermifuge* on Nosy. An' your last word shoulda been *invasion*, cause that little devil hit the ladder dead center."

"Well, I never," Velma exploded, "I'll bet the politicians love you. You vote a straight ticket every time. Nosy nearly kills you and you still stand up for him."

The Poacher

Al Payton, the forest ranger, happened by and was visiting Velma and Bill. As he sat on the edge of the back porch, he kept an eye on the calf moose over on the edge of the timber close to the road. His hot-blooded saddle horse, tied to a tree, had just clipped the sniffing Nosy with a quick hoof. The baffled moose backed up into the shadows of a big spruce. His spindly mane was standing erect, and he was stamping with his front feet.

As Velma came out of the kitchen to refill the coffee cups, a new car drove up and stopped with an important flourish. A flashy dressed man stepped out, leaving the car door open. When the three friends saw who it was, they sort of stiffened up, but put on their best grins when the man dressed up in the cowboy uniform walked over and shook hands all around and pulled cards out of his pocket. About then, the ranger saw the calf moose leave the unfriendly horse and walk over to the shining car.

Duke Johnson had spent many hours practicing his acts before a big private mirror at home. Now he picked out the one that fitted this kind of local yokels. No use to waste the best acts in his political poke on country people.

"Of course, you good people know I'm running for State Senator." He tilted his big William J. Bryan hat back on his noble forehead and poked a fat cigar in his mouth. "Now, I know you folks are *for* me, but I just dropped by to remind you it's getting toward voting time." Velma's ear drums thrummed as she went back into the house for another coffee cup. The town sharpie talked on and on about the great platform he'd erected. "I want to congratulate you forest ranger fellers on the fine job you're doing, Al." A pudgy finger snapped a blob of cigar ashes off his bay window. It lit in Bill's eye, but Patrick Henry didn't notice. He had his bulging peepers up on the high peaks of achievement. "But some other things in these parts I'm going to change. I know that the more important guides and out-fitters, and like Ol' Bill here, are with me, and the people are standing squarely behind me, when I re-organize that coffee-coolin' game department."

As the hot-shot garage owner adjusted his string tie, he didn't notice the sly grins exchanged by his restless audience. His ardor didn't arouse any enthusiasm in anybody except Al Payton. When the sharp-eyed ranger saw the calf moose hop in the open door of the car and disappear, he gave Duke Johnson a big handshake and said, "We're for you, Duke, give the big game poachers the works."

Nosy, busy chawing away on the head of lettuce, thought that this rubber-tired chuck wagon looked interesting. He hadn't yet had time to investigate the rest of the groceries on the back seat beside him.

Duke Johnson figured he had the upper end of Roaring River Valley all sewed up. So he shook hands again, and was soon headed, hell for leather, down the country. The politician, deep in his hazy cloud of heaven for all hands, hadn't noticed the long-nosed grafter in the back seat of his glory wagon. The hell-fired takeoff threw Nosy on the floor and the whanging bumps of the rocky road kept him from getting up. The calf was soon lying flat, and he was a very car-sick moose. The ranger knew he was the only one in the crowd to see the long-nosed boarder get on the gravy train, so just after Duke's car disappeared down the road, Payton stood up and said, "Bill, I see you got your telephone put in. Do you mind if I use it for a minute or two?"

"Help yourself, Al. Call up the State House and tell 'em we done elected the new senator."

Soon Velma and Bill could hear the ranger talking to somebody, and there seemed to be a lot of laughing on the country line. Al stayed awhile longer, then he stepped on his horse and rode off. Nobody missed the moose. He was in Velma's doghouse again. He'd chewed up a lot of the iris plants flourishing by the house, so Velma had put the run on him with a strong club. Bill and his wife figured Nosy's latest lumps had driven him down to the swamp behind the springhouse for his own private meditations.

When the two-legged grafter jerked the car to a stop, the four-legged one next to the back seat was deluged with the rest of the groceries. But the angry driver didn't hear the noise. He viciously jerked his big hat down and opened the door.

Just in front of him was a game warden's pickup parked squarely across the road that led to the ranger station and the town just below. One game warden sat on the running board reading a paper. His pardner got out of the cab and came over to grin at the angry politician. "Duke, old boy, sorry to git in your way, but we're lookin' for poachers."

"Look here, smart guy, you go polish up your badge with some

68

Gave a lusty squeal.

other cute jokes. I'm in a hurry and got no time for foolin'." Duke Johnson had caught too many fish several years ago. He still smarted from the small fine he'd got, after being caught by this particular warden.

"OK, OK, now keep your britches on, Duke." The other game warden was now leaning against the car fender. "We know that you're running for senator, and *if* you git in you'll make a good one, and mebbe some good laws. But we can stop any suspected poacher with the ones we got now."

Johnson burned a deep purple and started to splutter about damned smart alecks holding up decent citizens. "When I get in office, I'll put a stop to you badge-happy birds. You can't pull any funny stuff with me." The long-nosed grafter in the back seat had now got his sea legs, so he scrambled up, shoved his messy smeller under the back of Duke's big hat, and gave a lusty squeal. The cigar stub Duke swallowed before he jumped out of his car didn't make him half as seasick as the roaring laughter of the two game wardens.

The bog trotter scrambled out of the same door he'd went in, and was off at a grumpy trot up the timber fringed road towards Bill's ranch. The maybe senator crawled out from under the game department pickup, where he'd dived when the calf moose had told him off. Popeyed, the politician stood staring up the road as his short-tailed prisoner made his escape. Duke's new hat lay crumpled on the ground and the fancy cowboy uniform was smeared with dusty grease. Johnson had never heard of Bill and Velma's pet moose, and the whooping game wardens didn't tell him.

Slim Atkins rubbed his badge and told his pardner, "My gosh, there goes our evidence, and we caught old Duke red-handed, too." They got into their pickup and got out of the way. As Duke drove his car past them, he heard Slim, "I don't believe he'll cut the mustard. It takes a real poacher to make a good Senator." The flustered driver rammed his car down the rocky road, smarting at that last jibe. But what really boiled his radiator was that he couldn't put his finger on the frame.

Jam Session

It was later in the fall when the calf moose showed up again. Velma and Bill thought that the swamp angel had finally gone back to his own kind. They were much relieved at his absence, and so was the white collie. It was peaceful again.

In October, Velma and some other ranch wives had been down to the lower country, gathering buffalo berries. Now she had pots and pans filled with sugar, pulp, and berries, in the process of making jam for the coming winter. The hot stove was booming a tune with the sizzling juice and bubbling nectar. The tables and chairs were all occupied with glass jars and other containers, some full of this rich jam and some waiting. Bill was taking a rare nap on the old couch in the living room. He took time out, once in a while, to sniff the delicious odors from the busy kitchen. Velma was humming a tune in time with the bubbling jam, and had the jelly job about half done.

She heard some desperate whines, and in through the open kitchen door trotted Bill's shovel-nosed pet, his smeller decorated with a halo of porcupine quills. The moose calf skidded on the slick floor, Velma's hard-earned pride, and slid slam crash into the jam factory, head over tincup.

Electrified by the screams and squeals and crashing bangs, Ol' Bill bounced up and lit in the steamy kitchen to see a sight that durned near made him resolve to swear off making pets of the universe. His beloved wife and the glary-eyed moose calf were all sprawled out together in a conglomerate mixture of broken glass, mushy berries, and wine red jam spattering the kitchen landscape. The bog trotter's squealing mixed with Velma's screamed imprecations were more vociferous than articulate. When the bewildered hillbilly pulled his purple wife out from under the wreckage, the jam saturated moose blundered his needled nose out the door, leaving a trail of broken glass and crumpled aluminum kettles in his wake. His tracks dripped wine red clear up to the safer timbered hillside.

Just as Bill set the mumbling woman on her feet, the sourdough jar, teetering on the shelf above the stove, saw its chance and fell on poor Ol' Bill's gray head. Stunned, he sat himself down on a glassy space on the floor. He began wiping the yeasty sourdough out of his eyes, but he came out of his trance in a hurry when he heard two quick shots in the doorway. There stood his red-dappled

Levering another shell into his old rifle.

wife levering another shell into his old rifle, and taking a shaking aim out towards the peaceful mountain side.

Velma, stern-faced, lay at her silent ease on the old sofa in the living room. She had a copy of "Will Power and Its Influence on the Universe," and was all dressed up in her best clothes. The sound of scrubbing and polishing came from a disillusioned bowlegged man on his weary hands and knees. The kitchen was beginning to have a lived-in look, but a purple tinge still pervaded the edges of this food dispensary. Every time Velma heard the faintly mumbled comments from the kitchen, she had a little smirk all her own, remembering an old proverb, "Spare the rod and spoil the child."

Bill, now and then, would get up and go outdoors to shake the cramps out of his legs. Once he looked over and saw his pet in a willow bog below the corral. He had his schnozzle thrust into the black mud, and was very quiet. The skinny mountain man reflected that maybe he *should* teach Velma to shoot accurate, just maybe. She sure must have been excited, anyhow!

Ol' Bill went back into the kitchen and started scrubbing again.

The Clipper

The wind blowing past his sweaty head went on down the mountain carrying the message of U2, the best hair-growing oil in the world. Harry Clipper didn't know who would be interested up in this neck of the woods, or care. But his druggist friend down in Roaring River had assured Harry that the formula, concocted especially for the clipper, would even grow hair on Old Baldy, the highest peak on Roaring River.

The tired barber finally heaved himself off the log and started pussyfooting warily up the steep trail, careful to avoid breaking branches and rolling rocks. He kept traveling into the wind coming faintly out of the dark green jungle. Several times he swung around, his heavy rifle at the ready, but he couldn't see a thing. Maybe those muffled footfalls and low whines were his imagination working overtime.

Most everybody in the mountain town of Roaring River loved the barber. He had the only shop in town. This loquacious gent claimed to be not only the best tonsorial mechanic in the whole region but also one of the best hunters. Harry was an enthusiastic joiner of just about everything. He was a sucker for every hard luck ne'er-do-well in the country and was always broke. But that didn't hurt his ever present good nature.

Most of his customers enjoyed the tales of his hunting prowess. You could always spot the ones who had undergone his most vivid bear hunting adventures. No matter what their tonsorial preferences had been, they always sported crew cuts.

The trimmer was also an ardent member of the town's little theater group. His sonorous voice and theatrical gestures usually frightened new customers. Harry hadn't yet stabbed anyone, although some hardy souls admitted to some close shaves.

Of late he hadn't been chosen for any of the more juicy parts in the plays the L.T.G. had put on. The disappointed Thespian had put this down to his rapidly thinning locks, but by no means to any lack of histrionic ability. His generous use of the pungent hair remedy had shown, he thought, some remarkable progress on his re-seeding program. Also, the banker's wife, who was the main

74

director of the dramatic society and the Little Theater Group, had been less distant of late.

The clipper was sure he was staging a comeback. Besides, if he could manage to bag a big bull elk or some other large game, Clipper was sure that the entertainment department of his fleecing emporium would be well supplied for the winter season.

The spellbinder of the striped pole was thirsty. He'd gone some two miles from Bill Thompson's ranch, and although he'd seen what he was certain were fresh tracks and other sign of elk, he was sure he hadn't spooked any out of their beds. Pausing now in the shadows of the timber, he surveyed the spring-fed pool in the grassy park ahead.

Half a mile or so down the mountain below him the Forest Service had a plot with a high pole fence around it. The study of growth and general health of the infant spruce enclosed in this acre of reforestation had pleased the ranger in charge. The ranger hadn't yet found where an old-age pensioner pine in its second childhood had given up the ghost, but Bill Thompson's pet moose had discovered it. In falling, the huge tree had chosen to rest among the young spruce. Nosy had sneaked through the wrecked section of fence, and was gaily lunching on the tender crowns of the defenseless baby trees, when the shifting wind down the mountain wafted the delicious odor of U2 across his busy snout.

The druggist friend of the great Shakespearean actor was also the perfume supplier of most of Roaring River's elite. To give more authority to the trimmer's hair restorer, the astute pill roller had included some of the same scent that Minnie the schoolmarm used. Indecision wasn't a curse to the calf moose. When he got the message he suddenly deserted his salad buffet. He was now in a gallant trot up the mountain train, his anxious kisser wrinkling in happy anticipation.

Tom Worden, a former rancher with a natural flair for figures, including his wife's, had gotten into the banking business via her inherited cash and acquired culture. He could take the cash and let the credit go, that is when Esmeralda wasn't around. She had the curves, but Tom could pitch one when he had to. Since his wife had become the big shot in the Little Theater Group the banker loved to tease her with what he called *poetry,* but she sniffed it off as "sage brush vulgarity."

Mrs. Worden, looking for new worlds to conquer, decided it

would be fashionable to be a sportswoman. To set the pace for
her followers, she had acquired, "foah rathuh a neat sum," as she
put it, several distinguished outfits. "A hell of a lotta cash for
queer duds," Worden called it. When his wife proudly paraded one
of her more quiet outfits for the startled banker, he turned loose
what he termed a real prize:

"O them skin tight britches
An' real high boots
Don't b'long in ditches
Ner ol' tree roots.
A plumb red shirt
An' a real green collar —
I wouldn't kiss that flirt
Fer a whole half dollar."

When hunting season arrived, it didn't take much persuasion to
induce the banker to go big game hunting. In his time Worden had
done a lot of it. And secretly it amused him to suspect that Esmeralda
was disappointed when he agreed to go elk hunting. Tom was no
armchair sport but he knew an actress when he saw one.

They parked their car and horse trailer at Bill Thompson's ranch.
They'd have stopped to visit, since Bill was a long time friend of
Tom's, but nobody was home. So now they were riding up the
timbered trail looking for signs of game. Esmeralda spent so much
time admiring her shadow as she rode along that she was nearly
beheaded by low limbs. About the third time, Tom Worden
couldn't resist a new one. He said,

"If too much tuh eat
Is a plumb holy sin —
Then thuh low limbs'll beat
On that ol' double chin."

Mrs. Worden was about half mad at this crack and of a notion
to quit hunting, when a bull elk bugled in some close-by jungle.
The banker beckoned wildly to his pouting wife, stepped off his
horse, and started to tie him to a tree. He was pulling his rifle
from the scabbard when a big-headed old bull came charging out
into the small park. Esmeralda had gone deep into a dream of
playing the part of Diana the huntress when she was suddenly spun
into sad reality. Her old buckskin horse stampeded into the thick
timber fringing the park. The amorous bull had been hearing the
thumping hoofbeats and the stagestruck twittering of the huntress,
so he decided that here might be an orphaned harem. But he plowed

to a disillusioned stop between the two hunters. Old Tom had his rifle up and was about to pull trigger when he heard his wife holler and tough branches crack.

The banker was thankful, to say the least, when he found he'd forgotten to thumb the safety off. The bull whirled and escaped into the green jungle, and Tom discovered he was aiming his blunderbuss at the middle-aged spread of his screaming pardner. Her straining horse was wedged tightly between two trees, and Diana the H. held her arms high in the air, with the ends of the reins clutched tightly in her frantic fingers.

Later on, as they were riding farther on up the mountain, Worden couldn't resist saying what he claimed was an old mountain ryhme:

"When yuh're a-ridin' in thuh timber
Yuh gotta watch them knobby knees;
Sure you gotta be plumb limber
Or yuh'll knock down all thuh trees."

All he got was a dirty look from his Diana.

Just over a small ridge from where Tom and Esmeralda were hunting, the barber started to lean his rifle against a log and go over to the pond to get a drink, when he had a lucky thought. "Things could happen in a hurry," he mumbled. "I'd better cock this rifle to be ready." Harry had an uneasy feeling. He thought he'd seen a bear track close to the swampy spring. He pulled the hammer back on his rifle and leaned it against a fallen tree. He walked the few feet over to the swampy pool, then got down on all fours. He was leaning over to get a few swigs of mountain dew when he heard the long-drawn whines of some animal. "By golly, by dam, that's a bull elk a long way off."

The eager Clipper sat down in the tall grass and fished his new whistle out of his pants. "I'll just bugle him up and give him the medicine—if he's big enough." Harry tootled a few screechy calls and threw in some heavy Barrymore grunts for good measure. He listened some more. Sure that he heard some distant and stealthy sounds of approach, he was about to creep over and get hold of his ready rifle leaning on the deadfall, when he heard a disgusted grunt behind him and received a contemptuous bunt which tossed him head first into the mucky pool.

The banker's bull had forgotten the sashay with the two city slickers, and was busy venting his spleen on a small green spruce when he half heard the barber's hopeful tootling. Old Big Head left off slashing the tree, shook the sticky shreds of bark off his

77

massive rack, and started trotting through the timber towards the distant sounds. No tin horn could make sport of him, not the way he felt just now. An upstart younger bull with fancier footwork and some lucky jabs had run him out of the Buckskin Ladies Society a few hours ago, and here was some pipsqueak giving him the giggle. When the big elk ran out of the timber into the park, hellbent for election, he didn't see the running gear and hind end of Harry, struggling in the boggy pond. In his frustrated fury, all he could see was the disappointed little moose, walking away from the waterhole. "That's good enough," the old bull grunted. "No dern bog-trotter can make fun of me." Nosy just barely kept from sharing a muddy bath with Harry Clipper. He jumped over the fallen log just in time to dodge the charging elk. The calf's hind foot struck the barber's rifle, and when the gun went off KA-BOOM, that settled it. Nosy took off down the mountain in a frantic hurry. He didn't know that he was the only moose on Roaring River ever to shoot an elk in self defense.

Nosy was halfway to Thompson's ranch when the barber drug his miserable carcass out of the slimy water hole, to shiver and drip and stare at the last shudders of the bull elk's departure to the land of his fathers. Harry hadn't seen the pet moose and didn't know the bifurcated truth. So now he was forcing himself to believe that he had shot the bull before he had been shoved — fallen? — into the pond. Yes, sir, it just had to be that way? No bull. Oh, what a story to tell the boys. A sudden thought struck the barber, no bull? He ran over to the huge body of the fallen monarch draped across the deadfall. He kicked around in the broken and bloody branches and finally found his rifle. It was scratched up, but OK, with an empty shell in the chamber. Yes, he had shot the bull, no bull.

The exultant barber piled up some red-needled branches, fumbled around in his soggy britches for his waterproof matches, and soon had a fire going. After he had dressed out his elk and was more comfortable, he suddenly felt that he was the noblest Roman of them all, and that a speech was in order.

Esmeralda and Tom Worden heard the shot that killed the bull but couldn't tell the direction the sound came from. They had jumped a few elk but hadn't got a shot. Riding through some open timber, Tom, in front, reined his horse up short and growled, "Oh, that damned barber." He had once suffered a long bear story with a duck-tail haircut from Harry. The banker had a low opinion of Clipper, and what he saw now made him want to cry. The director of the dramatic society crowded her horse up close to Tom's when she heard him cuss.

The two elk hunters, looking past some tree trunks down into a small park, saw the mud-covered barber, facing away from them, standing with one foot on the bull elk's neck. He had his rifle lifted high in the air, and was declaiming to the sky.

While the astounded pair stared down at the barber, they heard him chant in a loud voice:

"Then out spoke brave old Harry,
　　The captain of his soul:
'Death cometh sooner, but barely,
　　To this elk of Jackson Hole.
But how can this bull die better
　　Than facing my fearless odds
For the ashes of his fathers
　　Amidst the temples of his gods?'
Mumble, mumble, mumble . . Lessee, now . . YEAH! this might fit—
What is there out beyond his grassy parks,
　　His yonder mountains with the snowy peaks?
O Bull, you've gone up your last trail,
　　Your pretty cows you've left behind,
I'll drink to you with that good old ale,
　　And hope you've joined up with your own kind."

A hungry horse fly lit on Worden's squirming neck and broke the spell up in the balcony. Tom slapped the pest away and happened to look over at his wife. Esmeralda, leaning forward in her saddle, was gazing raptly down at the orator, still waving his rifle and spouting to the universe.

Not to be outdone, the banker scratched at the flybite and came up with:

"He's noculated with uh phonygraph needle,
　　That barber is a plumb crazy fool.
Probly et uh rotten ol' beetle
　　Outa his musty ol' barber stool."

The entranced dramatic director didn't hear a word he said. She was still gazing awestruck at Clipper. So Tom reached over, pulled the horse's reins out of Esmeralda's unresisting hands, and rode off, leading the buckskin down through the aisles of timber. Diana hung onto the horn with both hands. But the show wasn't over, for Tom was mumbling to himself:

79

He was declaiming to the sky.

"C'mon, let's go,
Get away from here.
First thing yuh know
I'll shed uh tear.
C'mon, let's go.
We need some air.
Next thing yuh know
He'll kill uh bear."
It was getting along towards sundown as the banker and his wife
rode down off Bull Ridge to Thompson's ranch. The Thompsons
hadn't got home yet, but Nosy was there. When the hunters rode
over to the horse trailer and car, they saw the little elk killer up in
the horse trailer. He was licking at a lump of salt in a feed box.
He got peeved when Tom drove him out to make way for their
saddle horses.

"Oh, Tom, don't shove him," Esmeralda cried. "He's so innocent
and bizarre."

"Bizarre, hell," Worden grunted. Then he turned loose with:
"O little moose,
Don't look so sad.
It ain't no use
To be so mad.
Take out that snoot,
Go on, now git!
Or you'll have my boot
Right where yuh sit."

No Moose

Nosy's visits to the ranch in the next couple of years were rare. The only way you could tell him now from other bull moose was some deep scars on both front legs from a ruckus with a barbed wire fence. He was nearly forgotten now, except for occasional wisecracks aimed in Bill's direction by Velma or Tony when any moose were noticed close to the ranch.

This fall Thompson's hunting camp operated to full capacity, with Bill, Tony, and two other guides doing the work. Now the season was about over, the happy hunters departed with their trophies, and extra guides left for home. Old Bill and Tony were at the job of packing in some elk meat and gradually getting the camp back in to the ranch for the winter.

While Bill was arranging the sling rope on a pack horse, he noticed the wrangler. Tony was just leading a pack horse up to start loading some front quarters of elk. He stopped dead still and was looking at a mess of fallen timber close to the big swamp.

Thompson looked over the top of the pack-saddle. "What're you lookin' at, Tony, a grizzly?" Tony sniffed, "Naw, but I'll swear some silly ol' moose is followin' this pack outfit."

"Haw, haw, I'll bet it's that ol' gray moose that treed you. Prob'ly wants' t' return th' bridle she stole offa that buckskin horse you rode yesterday."

"Aw, go jump in the crick, yuh ol' moose lover." Tony glared around his droopy cigarette, and tied the pack horse up to a tree. "If y' wanta talk about moose, talk about 'em t'yourself, not t' me."

Just the day before, Tony had drowsed off to sleep while riding down the trail, having spent half the night looking for a lost horse. ("How did I know that nutty ol' buckskin would go right between a cow and her calf? Crazy damn moose!") His saddle horse stopped to graze. He wandered off the trail to work on some tasty grass in the fringe of heavy timber. What woke up the tired wrangler and the hungry horse was the furious mama. Maw had one front leg over Buck's mane in front of the saddle, and was coughing her snootful of slimy lily roots right in Tony's face. Her other front leg was twisted up in the bridle reins. The tangle of low tree limbs

82

this affectionate meeting took place under sure saved his life, according to cowboy Tony. "When that ol' fool horse started t'back up, I saw my chance and crawled up in that tangle o' branches. Ol' Buck let the moose have the bridle she'd pulled off, and went hellity larrup right back t'camp. Well, I stayed up there awhile after that dang crazy thing took off with her calf. Good thing camp wasn't far off. Tore a hole in my hat, an' my coat sleeve is ruined. Damn moose anyhow."

Bill rubbed some bloody scraps of elk meat on the bronc's nose. "There, that'll take th' scare outa him, and I'll betcha we don't even hafta tie a hind leg up."

The job was to pack out three bull elk that their hunters had killed the day before. The two gentlest horses were loaded by now with the bull Tony's hunter had got on a rough timber-covered hillside a mile above this big open park where the last two had been killed.

"Good thing it's level down here, an' easy footin," Tony said. "This wet snow is sure slippery."

"Don't look like these ponies ever been packed before." Bill Thompson had traded for these last four horses just a few weeks back. They seemed fairly well halter broke, and their saddle marks showed they'd been ridden.

After a lot of trouble Tony and Bill had three horses packed solid, with good diamond hitches pulled down hard on each one. Thompson was pulling the sling ropes tight on the last one. He didn't make a move till the wind came up. Then he got a whiff of the strong bull elk scent from the quarters he was loaded with. That bay rared straight up in the air, busting some branches on the tree he was tied to, then he fell down, got up, and tried to buck the pack off. He was cussing with bawling snorts and weird grunts. "Looks like he done lost his religion," says Tony.

The two packers were finally ready to go. They had tailed each horse to another's halter rope. These ponies would scatter their loads all over the mountains if turned loose to drive. "If you wanta go ahead," says Tony, "leadin' them two we packed first, Bill, I'll follow you. I'll show these four onery so-and-sos who's boss. I'm onery, too. If I git in a jackpot, I'll holler."

Bill was on his big black saddle horse, leading his two meat horses. They were tied head to tail and were gentle. "Good thing it ain't far t' th' ranch, with this setup. I'll travel up ahead aways,

Buck let the moose have the bridle.

an' if I hear any hollerin' I'll come help yuh, Tony. I'll keep any moose outa yer way, mebbe!"

Bill looked back after they'd lined out on the trail. Tony rode along, with all four meat horses walking head to tail and acting like old timers at the game. After about four miles of easy going in open timber, it started snowing hard. Bill's horses were traveling right along, so he pulled up until Tony, with his string, showed up.

"We're doin' OK, Bill." Tony was having trouble rolling a dry smoke in the gusty snow. "These here four broncs act like old hands."

Bill looked at the sidehill ahead and said, "I'll wait for you at the top of the clay slide, Tony. This wet snow ain't goin' to help the footin' on this greasy trail." Tony waved a wet glove, so Bill rode up ahead with his two pack horses.

The tromped-down trail that led up the clay hillside was a soggy mess of slippery horse tracks. There were lots of badger holes along the steep side. Up above the clay slide was a fringe of heavy timber. Down below, where the old clay slide had stopped, the timber and big rocks along the Shoshoni River was a jumbled-up bad dream of huge tree roots and snaggy poles all mushroomed together.

Just as Bill's outfit topped the trail and was heading into the timber he heard a big yell. It was from Tony. His outfit was about half way up the slippery trail and he was in trouble. Bill knew there was no room for his horse on that narrow trail, so he jumped off and tied the string of three to a tree. As he started running down towards Tony a bull moose trotted past him and disappeared into the spruce jungle. He was grunting his love call but Bill didn't appreciate it. Slipping and sliding, he passed Tony's saddle horse, who was just about pulled off the trail. This snorting and heaving tailed-up string of struggling horses was a soggy sight. The wrangler and his saddle horse were both trapped by his lead rope. It was clamped down under his horse's tail and tied to the string of pack horses behind him.

A horse packed with hind quarters of elk had slipped off the trail and was pulling the horse he was tailed to off with him. The meat horse behind him was braced stiff-legged in the trail, head and neck stretched out like a giraffe. The whole outfit was having a ring-tailed fit. Tony was so busy he could only grunt and cuss.

Bill climbed up opposite the helpless pack horse in the middle. He pulled out his hunting knife and whacked off the lead rope and then the tail rope. The freed pack horse went rolling and plowing down the steep hillside toward the jumble of big rocks and crazy upended tree roots at the bottom. Bill could hear his despairing grunts and crunchy thuds. Looking up the trail, Ol' Bill saw that Tony had come out of his jackpot and was OK. The last two pack horses hadn't made a move. Bill led them, walking behind Tony and his lead horse up the hill.

After they'd tied up the horses to trees alongside Bill's at the top of the trail, they floundered down afoot through the heavy timber fringing the clay slide. Bill said, "If this horse is still in one piece after this trip, he's a tough one." There was the pack horse at the bottom, a-laying on his pack of elk meat. His feet were trapped in a tangled up mess of roots and broken off stumps of upended spruce. This muggy dish was garnished with big blobs of snowy clay and chunks of shale.

"He ain't dead," Tony said, "but how in the devil are we goin' ta get him outa here?"

"We can cut the latigoes and lash ropes." Bill got out his knife and started in. The horse of many brands rolled free and staggered to his feet, trembling and heaving. "I'm goin' t'call him Lucky." The horse wrangler led the bruised-up horse over to the timber edge. "By golly, Bill, he's jist as spooky as ever, don't hardly even limp. Tougher'n a moose, he is. Dang ol' fool, I'm bunged up worse'n he is." Tony led him over to a tree and tied him up. "Musta been protected by all them brands he's plastered with."

"Or that tough ol' bull elk he was surrounded with," Bill put in. When the packers looked over the wreck, all that was busted up was the pack saddle. The heavy saddle pads, the elk meat, the cape, and the canvas pack cover had cushioned the rolling horse. Tony got out his tobacco and rolled a smoke, while Bill looked up the trail the horse had left when he rolled. "Them churned up furrows of mud an' rocks looks like a drunk bull-dozer went on a spree."

With one thing and another, Bill and Tony finally got the meat outfit in to the ranch. That night, Bill asked, "What caused all the ruckus, Tony? Don't tell me a moose done it."

"It's a short story," said Tony. "Th' truth is, it was my own damn fault. I just had t'have a smoke. In tryin' t'find a dry match, I needed both hands. So I thinks, everything is goin' fine, we ain't far from camp. So I *looped* the lead rope t'my saddle horn, and found *two* dry matches stuck together at the tip. When I scratched 'em on the brass screw on top o' my saddle horn, they sounded like Custer's last stand. It spooked that wringtail I was ridin'. He jumped, clamped his tail on th' rope, an' bogged his head t'buck. About that time I

86

Bill climbed up opposite the helpless pack horse.

was kinda busy, but I can figger what happened (hell, no, I couldn't look). My buckskin horse musta crowded my lead pack horse, who musta kicked th'horse tailed t'him. That's ol' Lucky. The horse tailed t'him musta got bit by the horse he was tailed to. Then ol' Lucky many Brands, with no other place t'go, plunged off the trail and you seen th'rest. I gotta admit it for once. It wasn't no moose. It was me. An', Bill, from now on, I ain't loopin' no lead rope over anybody's saddle horn. Not after this!"

Bill Thompson looked at Tony Belknap a long minute. Finally, "Tony, if I hadn't seen jist about th'whole deal, I'd a believed you read it in one a them dang magazines yuh pack around."

Old Gray Moose

Tony was a terrified ten feet up in the snaggy dead tree before a limb stopped him. The roaring grunt that lit his short fuse was coming from the same big moose he'd put his hard twist necklace on an hour before. When she rared up and clawed at the tree trunk with her sharp toes, the scared horse wrangler tried to climb higher, but a sharp snag spearing through his mackinaw pocket stopped that.

When Tony Belknap broke off branches and threw them at the glary-eyed moose, she didn't scare a durned bit. The bog trotter would just bunt at the tree, then strike at it with her strong front feet. Every time she would paw at his roost, the tall tree would sway like the town drunk. The wrangler suddenly decided to quit throwing limbs—he realized that sometimes tree roots have trench mouth; but that big-nosed devil didn't look like any dentist he'd ever come across.

The big gray cow was at the end of Tony's own rope. He could even see the stub of the corral post, with the spiked ends of broken poles, snubbed tight in a huge willow clump. But she had slack enough to give her treed friend the shivering tantrums. Tony figured that if he did sneak down, the foot-deep crusty snow wouldn't allow any quarter-horse speed, and his snooty jailer would stomp him in a hurry.

She stood quiet for a while, then she remembered past wrongs and glared up at him and stomped at the tree. She found the gunnysack with the horse bait close by the tree hole. She rared up and pounded it to shreds in a squealing rage. Her shivering prisoner realized that the passionate regard she had for him wasn't the kind of affection he cared for, so he hung on to his splintery snags a little tighter. I sure wish I'd opened the gate 'n' let 'er out 'steada ropin' th' damn thing," Tony chattered to himself. "Looks now like the best I kin git outa this deal is th' worst of it."

When the horse wrangler had found the cow moose in the old horse corral, he knew she'd jumped in over the top to get at the little pile of native hay he'd put in for his wrangle horse. Bill Thompson wouldn't be back to the ranch till night with the elk meat he was going to pack in. With the boss gone, Belknap figured it was up to him to teach one old swamp angel a thing or two. He tied the end of his saddle rope to the top of a corral post, got up on the top pole where he could make

89

a good cast, and throwed a big loop. Tony caught the moose right snug around her short neck. When she hit the end of the hard twist rope, the post busted off at the ground, and that part of the old corral caved in.

He got back out of the way of the stampeding moose all right, but he sure was mad when his forgotten wrangle horse ran out of the connecting corral and followed the cow moose. The wheezing bog trotter was making good time down through the willow swamp. The corral post stub with a couple broken pole ends attached would hit in the crusty snow, then fly high in the air. The big black horse veered off down through the timber one way, and the moose kept a snow-clouded fast gait the other, squealing every jump.

The cursing rope-happy gent realized he was afoot, the horse bunch was three or four miles down the river, and a foot of crusted snow to travel in. He darn well knew that when Bill rode in and found him afoot and what happened, that would be a fool thing that Tony would never live down. So he got a roped halter and threw it over his shoulder, threw a couple feeds of grain in a gunny sack, and started plunking off across the meadow. The wrangler figured he'd find the horses and oats-talk some pony up to easy reach, then drive the horse bunch in bareback.

Tony mumbled a couple of stumbling miles crunching down through the timbered parks, and now he could hear faint sounds of horse bells. He was just passing a big dead spruce in the middle of a willow park when it happened.

Tony didn't dare move. At least, he didn't think so. For when he even tried to shrug the cold off, the ancient spruce would sway a little, just a little. And the old swamp angel would come over, grunt a mean howdy, and paw at his roost if he made a small movement; that made the old spruce sway, too. The man in the tree house got cold. He got numb. Awful damn cold. His tight-fitting cowboy boots had overshoes, all right. "But did Admiral Byrd wear them things? Hell, no!" thinks Tony. "They ain't meant fer climbin' trees either, but here I am. Damn it. Damn all moose anyhow!" He thought, when the gray-coated bitch of a jailer lays down ta rest, he'd sneak down real easy, yeah, real quiet, then run like the devil.

Well, there she was, bogged down at the bole of the tree in her snowy bed, nodding her big dumb head. Tony's rope was even quiet. That manila collar he'd laid on her short hairy neck wasn't even moving. He waited, colder'n hell. He waited some more. Tony wondered if moose snore. Then she did. It was like a signal. Tony was ready to make the jailbreak. Just about that time here come three big blowzy ravens and lit on different limbs above him. Their beady eyes surveyed him, and one of the big birds said, "Caaw!" The snoring jailer whined up out of her sleep and lunged at the tree. Scared Tony into hollering. The dead tree weaved like a broken down ferris wheel, but Belknap didn't enjoy the circus, not that one. But those ravens did. They gave out with a lot of gurgling caw, caws. When they jumped off their snags at the top of the tree to flop on their way, the leverage they had at the crown made the wrangler hate roller coasters, too. Did that spruce weave then, and sway!

Mr. T. Belknap got so scared he got warm. Then Old Snouty walked over six or eight feet and lunched on some willows. As she flopped her big upper lip around the moose macaroni and snapped it off, she'd roll her eyes up at the wrangler and give a moany wheeze. The hard twist necklace made her fidgety as it got in her way. Tony knew by that time that moose have a single-track mind, and he was on the main line. Every time he'd move a numb foot or blink a cold eye, she'd stop crunching and look up at him and squeal. Just a little, but enough.

The horse wrangler had cooked himself sort of a skimpy breakfast. Velma Thompson had left the ranch right in the middle of hunting season to take care of her sick sister Minnie. Ol' Bill was a pretty good substitute cook, but now he was gone, too. Tony was feeling sort of empty, now, in more ways than one. The sun warmed him quite a bit. But now it started to cloud up a little. What sun he could see was on the opposite side of the tree from him; and he was a little leery of getting on the sunny side, because any movement enraged the moose and jittered the spruce. Tony said feebly, "Damn moose ta hell, anyhow!"

The sun came back and warmed him a little, but the breeze that came with it swayed his tree so much that Tony wished he'd gone to church that Sunday he'd been in town with the boys. He remembered that his mother had warned him long ago that little boys playing with ropes sometimes came to bad ends. Yes, that was long, long ago.

Mr. Belknap got so cold he got sleepy, but when he woke up with a moosemare, so did his snooty pardner. After she quit cussing him in her whiny language, Tony thought of the life jacket he had hung on his shivering withers. He slowly got the halter off his shoulder, and finally got its rope around the big tree trunk, and fumbled it around his body in a loose knot. "If I go to sleep or freeze, that moose won't git me," he whispered to himself. "If this blamed tree falls, I'll go

91

down with the ship." His thoughts must have got to the cow, for she gave him a swampy sneer and the coarse hair of her mane stood up. She stomped on the snow, and her tongue ran in and out under that floppy nose.

The cold man in the tree had a glimmer of hope once. The bog trotter moved around to get some fresh willows. She twisted up the stiff saddle rope into a kink. It was wet and half frozen, and she mistook part of it for a willow stem, and flopped her lip around it. As she closed her jaws down, Tony, watching in frantic hope, thought, "This is it! She'll free herself now, and pull outa here." When his captor gave a disgusted grunt and spat the rope out unbroken, Tony B's heart nearly failed.

Time wore on. The moose laid down and chewed her cud. Then she got up and walked around in the hard-cased snow till she came to the end of Tony's best rope. Then she wheezed an angry squeal and glared up at the freezing wrangler. He said to himself, "When I die and go to"—he then remembered some of his past life—"well, wherever I go to, I sure hope there ain't no onery moose there."

Finally it got dark, and Tony figured maybe moose can't see at night. So he made some quiet and stealthy descending moves. He discovered that this one could see better at night than daytime. After the tree quit swaying and the swamp angel quit pawing it, the clouds moved over and let the moon come out. About that time some big whirring bird lit in the crown of Tony's private spruce, flopped its heavy wings, and called, "Who, wha, hoo."

The gray moose wheezed and crunched away from the tree a little. The big horned owl would peer down and holler, "Hoo, ha, hoo, hoo," then flap its wings and make the tree sway, just enough to give Tony the hooting d.t.'s.

Just about the time the miserable, half-frozen man decided he'd let go all holts and let the owl finish up what little the cow moose left on the ground, he heard some horse sounds from over in the dark timber toward the main trail. Tony took a chance that it was Bill coming back from camp. He yelled, the big gray jailer gave a coughing grunt and pawed the tree, and the big owl hoo-hooed the very idea.

It *was* Bill, and he hollered back and rode out into the moonlit park. The big gray moose got scared, and when she hit the end of Tony's rope, it broke where she'd chewed it, and she was gone, hellity lick, down through the black timber. Tony couldn't get down out of the tree, he was so cramped and numb. When Bill helped him down, Ol' Bill said, "If ya want me ta help git your big-eyed friend outa the top

92

She remembered past wrongs.

a your·playhouse, you'll have ta wait till mornin'." The horned owl flapped his·wings, the tree swayed, and both men crunched away from there fast. "Hoo, ha, hoo, hoo!"

The Ridin' Moose

The only thing that kept the pack horse from sinking deeper was
the flat bottoms of the rawhide panniers slung under the top pack.
Tony and Bill were in the process of getting the last of the pack and
camp outfit back to the ranch when this had to happen.

"Ease up a bit on that rope, Tony, I gotta tie this pole under his
tail ta hold him steady." Bill was spotted with blobs of slimy clay,
and wet from his hips down to his boots, half sunk in the litter of
broken up green spruce branches and splinters of shattered poles that
used to bridge the boggy part of the trail crossing the moose swamp.

Tony jabbed lightly with his spurs. His apaloosie gingerly stepped
up a few inches, his feet sinking in the blubbery mess of swamp grass
on the edge of the dense timber. The wrangler kept his tight rope
dallied around the saddle horn to keep the bogged pack horse from
struggling deeper into a maybe grave. The mud-splattered packer cut
the pack rope. He finally heaved, hauled, and slid the tent top pack
and the grub-loaded panniers to safety on higher ground.

After the trail pardners drug the pack horse out and reloaded the
cargo on the shivering animal, they stopped to take a rest. Tony licked
a cigarette together, and let a couple dribbles of smoke out of his bony
beak. "You shore don't look like any creasy pants dude I ever seen,
Bill. Them spots of mud make you look like a messed-up apaloosie.
My horse is gonta be jealous."

Bill was scraping the slimy mud off his mackinaw and leather chaps
with the back side of his hunting knife. The rest of the loaded pack
string and Bill's saddle horse, all tied to trees bordering the park, interrupted his answer to Tony's jibe by snorting and raring back on
their halter ropes. Just about then a big cow moose, followed by her
awkward knobby-legged offspring, trotted out of the timber.

The old mamma moose didn't look right or left. She just trotted
right through the soggy hole recently inhabited by the pack horse, and
was successfully followed by her offspring. They disappeared in the
jungle of swamp-rooted trees. "That danged old bog trotter didn't
even hesitate, Tony, and look at the hell me and that horse went
through in that mudhole. Yeah, you helped, but that there horse and

95

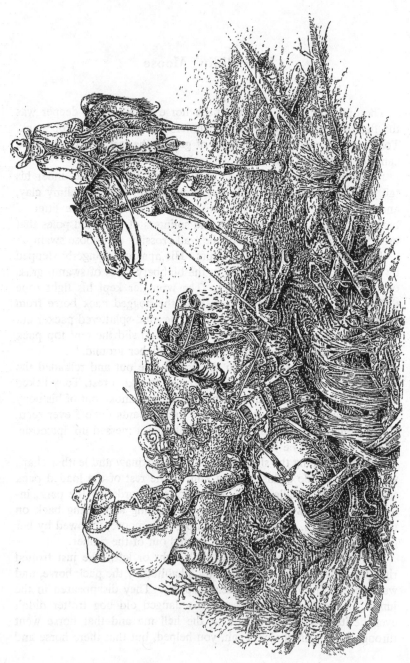

The guide kept his tight rope dallied.

me shows who done the work. Now, like I've always said, we oughta ketch us a few moose, and break 'em ta ride 'n' pack."

"Yeah," said the horse wrangler with heavy sarcasm, "you showed your style of moose-ridin' last trip." Bill's hunter had apparently killed a big bull moose. The guide walked up to the huge prostrate body and prodded it with a long pole to see if life was extinct. He thought it was, so he leaned his rifle against an old deadfall, straddled the body, and was trying to pull it over on its back to start dressing it out. The hunter, meantime, was focussing his camera on Bill's struggle to get set. He was flabbergasted to see the big bull suddenly revive and carry Bill, riding backwards, off into the timber at a staggering run. When his guide came back out of the timber, ragged and skinned up, and wobbled over to the horses, he was in no mood to listen to the photographer's excited claims about the best action shots ever produced this side of Hollywood.

"That there ride was different," Bill protested. "That bull didn't know what he was doin'. I think if a feller would ketch 'em young and train 'em right, it could be done. If that pet Nosy had stuck around, I'd a tried it on him." Tony the moose hater snorted and half swallowed his cigarette. Between gulping coughs he got out, "Yeah. You and them funny ideas. That bear cub you tried t'teach how t'track elk last fall'll do me. The bacon grease you spilled on your britches dang near caused you t'be th'only one-legged bear trainer in Jackson Hole."

The guide knew that his horse-wrangler friend detested moose. After he'd been treed for five or six hours by a cow moose he had a healthy fear of them. Bill liked to dig him about his prejudices. They got on their horses and started to drive the pack string up the trail when Bill jabbed him again: "Tony, I was readin' a book the other night. A famous natcherlist claims that moose *have* been trained ta ride 'n' drive."

The wrangler spurred his horse into a trot to get ahead of the pack string. His parting jibe was, "If ya don't quit readin' them ol' books, ya'll git as loony as th'guy that wrote 'em."

Ol' Bill, back at the tail end of the bobbing string of pack horses, grinned to himself in the cold and growing darkness. He couldn't glimpse his jittery friend away up in the lead. The tree-lined trail twisted up the steep timber-covered mountain. But he caught a few stray whiffs from the wrangler's homemade cigarettes. "Ah ha," the guide thought, "Tony's smokin' t'keep himself company. Figgers th' dang smoke screen'll keep th' devils away, especially th' willow

97

Carried Bill, riding backwards.

crunchers." The clip-clop of iron shoes and an occasional snort as some low branch scraped on a pack cover was the only noise. Horses traveling mountain trails at night seem to forget grudges. They are luxuries for the daytime, but all enemies are friends in the dark. Going up the switchback trail, they jumped two or three elk, but had no trouble. As they came out into the parks below the ranch, two moose cows and a calf were feeding in a small beaver pond full of slough grass. Bill saw them outlined in the frosty moonlight, against the silvery aspen hillside above them. They just raised their long dripping snouts to watch, and never made a move.

The two men got their pack horses into the corral and went to unpacking. After Tony and Bill grained the horses, they saddled a couple of fresh ones and throwed the whole tired string down in the timbered parks to graze for the night. They put their wrangle horses in a small side corral, gave them hay for the night, and headed for the bunkhouse for supper. After Velma had left, Bill and Tony had sort of let things get cluttered up around the home cabin. So they had taken to using the old bunkhouse. Their domestic disorders were less easily detected and the housekeeping was simpler.

Tony was reading a dog-eared old pulp western, his big hat tipped over close to his long bony nose. He'd read this one five or six times, but it was his favorite. The rickety old bunkhouse had lost a lot of the clay daubing in between the logs, and Tony sat close to a crack you could throw a cat through. He was used to breezes so he was reading one.

His pardner Bill was hunched over a tattered old dictionary, propped up by a couple pieces of split pine stove wood laid on the shaky-legged board table. He detested the sight of the pile of gaudy western magazines stacked in the corner by the horse wrangler's bunk. Bill had to read the dictionary as this was the only other printed matter he could find. Reading can labels was out, he'd memorized all of them, from Alphabet Soup to Zedder's Baked Beans. Besides, he was finding words that would come in handy on onery horses and locoed horse wranglers.

Maybe that contrary college professor he guided on the last trip had done him a favor. This cubic foot of words might turn out to be the best tip he'd ever got from any egocentric big game hunter.

Tony was leaning over his tale in literary ecstasy. Just as Wild Bill Hiccups was drawing a bead on the last of the brawlin' Balton boys, the old pillow fell out of the busted window pane back of his tensed head, and a long bulbous snout reached in to caress the black hat brim, and pushed it on to Tony's nose. The startled cowboy came out of his dreams of the Hokay Corral, and turned to stare into the curious eyes of a maudlin moose. He fell over backwards with an uncowboyish squawk of terror, shoving the senile table against the serious Websterian scholar. Down went Ol' Bill on the floor with the wrecked table. The coal oil lamp lost its smoky glare of competence; and when the cork let go in the bowl, the flame joined forces with John D.'s product, and lit the little old log shack of intellect with a snaky blaze of fiery exuberance.

Bill's hairy paw clutched the professor's wordy book for a new slant on education. He got up in a singed rush and made for the door. He put one shoe-pack on the prostrate wrangler's belly in his stampede, but got the door open, and galloped out of the lit-up house of learning. He grabbed a shovel leaning up against the cabin, and began throwing snow inside to douse the fire. The first shovelful hit Tony in the face, ker-whunch, as Tony groaned to his feet. The next few cooled the fire, but met obstacles being thrown out of the cabin. Tony was bent on saving the Balton Boys and all their enemies from the flames.

Finally the fire sizzled out. The two tired students got another lamp from the cabin behind the bunkhouse. Bill found his dictionary in the snowbank just outside the door. But poor Tony found his best magazines in a pulpy mess, half burned and half soaked, where Bill's shovel had ricocheted them back into the fire.

The men straightened up the wrecked table and battered chairs. Tony examined what was left of his library.

"Bill, you musta been th' star batter when you was a kid. Yuh batted my readin' right back inta the fire when I was a-tryin' t'save some o' the best."

"Now that there is gratitude fer yuh!" Bill snorts as he is sweeping up the glassy wreckage off the singed floor. "Save your life, and you kickin' about them dog-eared old westerns."

Tony piled the remains of his classics into a safe corner and helped clean up the mess. Then they decided to hit the hay, the class was over. Bill's bunkful of blankets had escaped the soggy snow. Tony shook out his wet blankets and finally crawled into his damp bed. He groaned all night. His belly hurt where the bowlegged fireman had stomped, and from the loss of Gray Zane's best. The triumphant fireman slept good. He had his dictionary safe under a dry pillow. Bill woke up just once. That was when poor Tony was having a wild dream about a moose that was chewing on some of his pulpy literature.

100

Before sunup next morning Bill heard Tony outside the bunkhouse mumbling to himself. He remembered the ruckus last night, and figured Tony hadn't had too good a sleep. He dressed and popped his head out the door. There was Tony, moon-eyed and grumpy from a poor snooze. He had one end of a saddle rope tied to a tree about seven feet up, and was just jerking the rope tight to another one about thirty feet away. "Gotta dry them blankets out. That snow you throwed on 'em last night wet 'em up. I'll hang 'em up after we wrangle horses."

"Man, I'm glad yuh put that rope high enough so it don't ketch a feller under the chin," says Bill, buckling his chaps on. "I knew a gent once who was kinda in a hurry one night. He run his horse under a clothes line. It caught him in the Adam's apple. And bein's that his boots hung up in the stirrups, that bird's career is now bein' pursued down yander. Knowin' this guy pretty well, it's a cinch he ain't up above."

It was getting a little lighter in the sky by the time they ran the horses in from the grassy parks below the cabins. Bill shut the corral gate on the last of them. Tony, still groggy from his dreams, stepped off his mount. He uncinched his horse and was looping the latigo up on the rigging ring, when Bill hollered. The horses were all running frantically around the corral, trying to get away from something black moving along in their midst.

Tony forgot his dangling cinch and stepped up on his horse to get a higher look-see at what all the commotion was about.

Bill was on his own horse. He yelled, "There's a dang ol' moose in there. I'll open th'gate 'n' let 'em all out. We c'n git rid o' th'moose 'n' run th'horses back in!" He leaned from his pony, slid the pole lock back, and swung the gate open. The nervous bunch of snorting horses streamed out of the gate, with a big bull moose following at a grumpy trot, his long bell swinging sidewise, with angry flourishes. Not wanting any more close association with a moose, Tony reined his high-withered nag around, and loped him off to one side, out of the way of the fast-running horses.

Bill galloped his horse up through the willows and bent the horses around to head them back to the corral—minus the moose, who faded away in the timber. It was light now. As Bill hollered at the reluctant horses he could see the horse wrangler riding fast on the far side of the loose bunch. He was just going through some high willows.

The thick mat of willows hid a trail through the bog. Tony was riding hell for leather to get around some loose horses. He was mak-

He automatically reached for a mane holt.

ing good time when his horse stopped short. The amazed wrangler lost his reins and grabbed the saddle horn with both hands. He sailed through the air, his cinch popping against his heavy chaps. When he lit, he found himself *still* in the saddle, and *still* going like hell. But it wasn't old Brownie he was on. From the squealing coughs and startled grunts, he knew dang well this must be a dream. He shut his eyes and hung on for dear life.

Those popping snores couldn't be Ol' Bill over in his bunk. It didn't smell like Bill, either. When the wrangler felt his saddle slip, he automatically, dream or no dream, reached for a mane holt. That's what woke him up. When his clutching fingers grabbed a handful of stiff, bushy hair, he woke up. Then what he saw made him shut his eyes plumb tight. "Ride 'er, kid. Ride 'er! Whoopee!"—Tony dimly hears Bill holler with wild enthusiasm. "Yuh made a good trade. Stay with 'er, Tony!"

"Oh, no! Traded ol' Brownie fer a moose?" Tony fearsomely opened one eye, then shut it quick. A moosemare for sure. The wind whipping past his dizzy head brought the bitter and musky smell of his fast-moving mount. He wanted to pinch his nose, but didn't dare let loose of her mane or the saddlehorn.

Tony was thankful he'd taken off his spurs last night. He was going to hell fast enough. About the time poor Tony was wishing he'd led a better life, he felt a terrible jerk on his brisket. He knew for sure it was the top pole of the Hokay Corral he'd hit. Then the lights went out.

Now Tony was afraid he was going to live. He was coming to. The wrangler's hand clutched the broken clothes line. He moved, then knew his back wasn't broke. He was still in the saddle, his other hand on the horn. . . . He felt a boot in the stirrup, oh, why was he born? . . . "Damn all moose, anyhow," Tony started to sneeze. . . . He lay back on the snowy ground, and felt the big breeze. . . . He stared up at Ol' Bill who knelt on his knees. . . . He was fanning the reclining wrangler with the professor's dictionary.

As the dazed wrangler sat up, close to the bunkhouse, he realized what had happened. "Yuh was doin' fine, Tony," says Bill, helping Tony get unscrambled from the saddle. "You ain't defunct, but yer deceleration was too durned expeditious."

Tony got up then, and muttered to his grinning nurse, "Aw, hell, take that damn dickshunary, an' go t'college!"

The Perfessor

For several winters a family or two of moose had wintered below town a few miles. There were some extensive willow flats along the river, and the snow didn't pile up enough to bother them. One cantankerous cow moose lost her bearings on her way to these winter quarters, and was hung up temporarily in a dense patch of willows and cottonwood trees just behind Minnie's house on the outskirts of Roaring River.

This long-nosed crosspatch was extra irritable because some boys had sicked their dogs on her the evening before, at a ranch above town. She had just about regained a full belly and enough aplomb to make a detour and continue her journey, when the retired schoolmarm came crashing through the tall willows. Old Minn was searching for Algernon, her Pomeranian pup. He was asleep in a safe corner of her back porch, but she didn't know it. She was in a hurry to shut him up so she could go shopping with her sister, Velma Thompson, and a friend.

The pup's scent on Minn's coat set the moose into a swampy rage. When the two crusty old maids met face to face in the willow clump, the one in the red coat gave an eighth grade screech and lit out for home. The longer-nosed one in the gray coat wasn't about to take any such mean remarks, so she started blowing snuffy insults right back and fell in behind. The school marm forgot all about the desk-bound arthritis in her joints when she came to the barbed wire fence she'd laboriously crawled through a few minutes ago. She went under the wire like a squatting thoroughbred. Minnie thought she'd won the race, until she heard her cantankerous contemporary bust through the barbed handicap and start to close up the snorting and breathless gap in between.

Just about to be overtaken, the ex-dictator of county education suddenly ripped off her crimson jacket. She threw it in the path of her opponent, who seemed about to win the election. This was no fixed race, but the cow moose suddenly plowed to a stop, and started to stomp on Minnie's jacket with her long front feet. Snuffy knew if she got the hide first, the carcass would come later.

Back at Minnie's house, Velma Thompson and her friend were still

104

waiting. The friend spied the old maid windmilling along in the distance. "Isn't that Minnie," she asked, "running over there?" Velma looked out the window. "Oh, no, that isn't her. Min can't go that fast."

The frantic woman was running to the nearest haven, her neighbor's house. They were just about to get into their car in the driveway, when Minnie came spurting around the corner and tripped over the man's legs. The heaving bundle of petticoats and old fashioned education banging up against his legs threw him in the open car door and against the horn button. The moose came pounding around the house at full speed, but was turned by the blaring horn and the screams of the two women.

The cow moose was back down in the safer willow clumps along the river. Minnie and her neighbors were inspecting the wreckage of the two moose-made gaps in the freshly painted picket fence enclosing the garden. The old maid had been revived to her usual vinegary humor, and she was now vowing that she was going to have vengeance on that cow moose, even if she had to use up all the wardens in the whole game department.

The new game warden had only been on the job a short while, but he had already been dubbed "The Perfessor." His talk of scientific game management, and his badge-heavy manner hadn't won him any trust or affection. Minn, hurrying up the main street of Roaring River next morning, nearly ran over the warden. He was adjusting his large hat in the reflection of the windshield of his new pickup parked in front of the post office. The post office door was open, and Minnie stuck her tongue out at the postmaster slyly peering out through his bars. These two old people had feuded ever since he had first pulled her braids in school. Then the schoolmarm crowded right up to the game warden and said, "Young man, I want you to do something about that mean moose in my back yard."

"Just what are you talking about, madam?" The perfessor gave her a quick once-over. He felt of his manly chin and straightened the collar of his well tailored red shirt. The sight of that red shirt made Minnie remember her own moosed-up coat. It got her dander up. "Now you listen to me, young man," Minn had her best long finger waving in front of the tall warden, "The cow moose that chased me through my own fence and wrecked my neighbor's fence has got to be dealt with."

A man in an old faded shirt and worn levis paused in the post office doorway with one scuffed boot on the threshold. He was intently

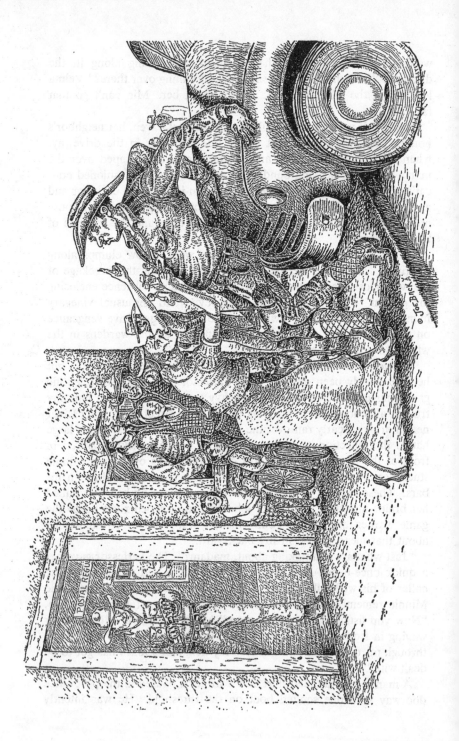

studying the wrapper on a tightly rolled newspaper, and appeared to be in a pleased dreamy trance. The bored game man yawned and started studying his highly polished fingernails. "What moose, lady?" A couple of kids parked their bicycles squarely in the center of the sidewalk and were listening with knowing grins, as Minnie, striving for control, got to going on her description of the happenings. Her voice got louder and louder. Now, other townspeople, young and old, most of whom well knew the old school superintendent, casually strolled by, or stood and studiously gazed up at Old Baldy, back above town.

The seething old maid finally got her story told to the disdainful game expert. When she had finished, he suddenly leaned forward, stuck both hands in his hip pockets, pushed out his well rehearsed jaw, and said, *"Who* do you think you're kidding, lady? Moose don't do *that!"*

"Don't *you* tell *me* what moose don't do." Minnie was now tapping her veteran finger on the shiny badge. The startled man was backed up against the hood of his official pickup. "I've seen hundreds of your kind. The back of your books are all worn out before you've ever seen the front. You *know* all the *answers*—but you JUST DON'T UNDERSTAND THE QUESTIONS!"

The game warden for once in his life absolutely didn't know what to do or say. The old school mom, who loved infighting, saw that she had the Perfessor punchy. The audience gathered around, enjoying the show, waited for the climax. So she gave him the old one-two. "Young man, you can keep your *degree,* but if *you* don't *do* something about that *moose,"* she had her jaw synchronized with her finger, "I'll have your badge pinned on *somebody* that's got more between the ears than *you'll* ever have!"

The old school supe punched a final period on his badge, shook her digit under the man's flustered nose, and marched into the post office. She glared at her schoolmate behind the bars, got her mail, and made a triumphant Carrie Nation march back to her home among the cottonwoods.

Minn learned from her neighbors that the warden spent the next day or so combing the willow clumps along the river back of their houses. The old cow moose had moved on, for the Perfessor hadn't contacted her or any of her kind, one neighbor reported.

The warden must have found out Minnie's relationship to Velma and Bill, and something about the pet moose. Velma told her sister that the game man was evidently very much offended at the public

107

lecture administered by Minn. He drove up to the Thompson ranch and accused Bill of keeping a game animal in captivity. And that, he reminded Bill, was against a state law.

"If you're thinkin' about that pet moose Nosy, mister, yuh've got another think comin'." Bill had heard about the new warden and wasn't impressed. "He ain't in captivity an' never was. Only time we ever see him any more is when he gets a notion to board off us for awhile. The game department owes me plenty for moose-boarding, if that makes yuh feel any better."

"Well, I've heard of you, Thompson, you and your pets," the Perfessor was miffed at Bill's lack of reverence. "I'll have you know I've got my eye on you."

The old guide had to laugh at that crack. "Well, well, warden, yuh *shore* make me jealous. Why, hell, man, *everybody's* got their eye on *you!*"

The Perfessor gave Bill his most scientific glare. Then he stalked over to his pickup and drove back down the road. Thompson soon got word on the grapevine that the expert had got his F.B.I. instincts aroused, and had confided to admirers that he was onto Old Bill. And that he was going to get evidence to cinch Bill's hide to the Game Department fence.

Nosy, off on some trip of his own, hadn't been around the ranch for quite a while. Velma tried to check up on him with Bill's binoculars. She reported that several times she'd seen a gaunt old cow moose with a pair of twin calves, hanging around up in the swamps above the ranch. "Those calves are sure cute, Bill," Velma said. "They're so fat, no wonder the old lady is so skinny. Once, I *think* I saw Nosy, trying to cut one out of the bunch."

Awhile later the rancher was up on the hillside above the buildings, checking on his water system. He cleaned some moss out of the spring. Now he was looking for a stick to scrape mud off the shovel. Seeing movement over in some close timber, he located two men walking through the trees. Their manner and gestures seemed furtive to Ol' Bill, so he walked over to stand behind the huge trunks of spruce trees for a closer look-see.

The old hillbilly soon recognized the men as the game expert and a man new to the country, who had started a gun and sporting goods shop a short time ago in Roaring River. The big game warden had a pair of field glasses slung around his neck by a long strap. He carried a large camera in one hand, and the other hand and arm were pointed down at the Thompson ranch buildings below them. The short four-eyed gent had a large long-snouted movie camera focussed down on the buildings. Bill could even hear the whirring clicks as the machine was turned slowly around. This man's pot belly was encircled by a wide, well-filled cartridge belt. From it a long barreled hog leg dangled in a huge holster.

Ol' Bill got kind of ringy at their sneaky actions. But he got so tickled he nearly gave himself away when the camera man fell down, tripped by his own heavy artillery. The Perfessor was directing the documentary film, and had his red clad official arm pointing down towards the ranch when the camera man tripped. Hollywood was trying to get to his feet from the mixture of swamp grass and tree limbs, when Bill saw two moose calves rise up out of the hiding place where maw had planted them. They were halfway between the two detectives, who hadn't been aware of them; but their mother was, and when she heard their moggy whines she nearly ruined Bill's new underwear. He hadn't seen her, nor did she see him, as she roared down past the big spruce Ol' Bill was so affectionately behind.

From her root-chewing station in the hidden bog above the spring, her snot-blowing whuffy charge brought maw moose dang near on top of the warden's head camera man. The only thing that saved him was the still whirring movie camera upended in the grass. As he dived under a snaggy deadfall near by, the infuriated moose started to stomp and pound Mr. Bell and Howell into a conglomerate mess of worthless evidence.

The Perfessor had been so fast getting up in the tree that the interested spectator peeking from behind the big spruce saw only a blur of red. But the movement had attracted maw even if she couldn't tell time. Like most people on their way up, the game warden had left something behind. It was his own private camera; and while it did save his life, he lost some skin where his hip pockets had been. The big cow was viciously clawing and spearing her front toes into the warden's camera, while he was vainly trying to climb higher up in the limby dead tree. The strong strap looped over his neck held his wildlife special binoculars tight under his pugnacious chin, while the encircling strap was hooked to a snag on the tree trunk. The cow moose got over her photogenic craze, and now turned her attentions to the struggling Perfessor. She had shoplifted one hip pocket with some epidermistic interest, and had inserted a slashing toe into the other, when the problem was solved by the breaking strap.

While the big bog trotter was settling her maternal difficulties with the game department, the bowlegged witness behind the tree enjoyed the proceeding and judged it a smashing success. Every time the game expert up the tree hollered to the picture expert under the tree to get his cannon and kill old Snuffy, the camera man would make an effort to crawl out to look for his lost six-shooter. The moose calves hadn't moved out of their tracks during the whole ruckus as maw hadn't told them to, yet. Whenever Hollywood made a move the kids told on him, being close by and squealers by nature. Maw spent the next few minutes commuting from tree to tree, until Nosy showed up and tried to make friends with the twins. That settled it. The snooty old female couldn't stand the idea of any delinquent contaminating *her* kids, so she run Nosy off down the mountain, and was soon leading her long-legged offspring out of such a gossipy and troublesome neighborhood.

Thinking that the show was over, and sure that neither of the treed men was hurt, Thompon was about to slip back unobserved down to the ranch buildings, when he heard some range cows bawling and some loud shouting. On the other side of the still waiting pair of treed men, a couple of unwilling white face cows and a calf came into sight. Through the open timber on the trail leading down the mountain, Bill could see his friend Tony Belknap riding along, hazing the range cows. Ol' Bill could see that the game warden and the camera operator were hiding from Tony, now. They were sure the cow moose had departed, but didn't want the cowboy to catch them in such tale telling circumstances.

One of the cows tried to break back up the country, but Tony spurred his horse and bent her back down the trail. The red shirt of the Perfessor up the tree must have caught the cowhand's eye, for he rode up for a closer look. He darned near got thrown off his startled horse when Hollywood crawled out from under his snaggy shelter to shake the kinks out of his carcass.

The hidden hillbilly saw Tony's mouth open as he held in his plunging horse. The cowboy finally took the picture in and got his wits about him. "Say, warden, mebbe it ain't any o' my business," Tony said, "an' yuh don't hafta tell me if yuh don't wanta, but what in hell are yuh a-doin' up that tree?"

As Belknap looked from one to the other of the strangely silent men, Hollywood got uneasy. He figured that the Perfessor was the cause of it all and knew all the answers, and should understand the question. He was just as dumfounded as the cowboy at the long pause.

"Yes, by George, *what am I* doing up this tree?" The Perfessor was staring down at the two men down below him. *"Me,* with my *education!* By golly, I quit!"

Bill Thompson had a silly grin on his face as he turned around and sneaked back down to the ranch house.

Washday Moose

Velma's numbed fingers fumbling a clothespin over a shirt were nearly torn off by the clanging wire. Looked along the jumping jacks of her freezing wash, she saw the huge maw crunch down on Bill's new levis. Turning in frantic haste to run towards the cabin, she caught up the big clothespin pail and took off down the shoveled path. The bull moose spat out his fresh chew, plunged around the rattling clothes and trotted easily through the snow in her wake. Velma, out of breath and overtaken, suddenly jumped into a deep snowdrift and instinctively pulled the pail over her head. Puzzled at the disappearance of his quarry, the bull plowed to a stop, took a good look at the pail bottomside up; and he reached his big smeller over to nose at the shaking metal. The freezing prisoner in the tin hat, hearing the breath of doom, gave a nervous sneeze and shoved the pail up in a desperate attempt at escape.

Down in the corral, Bill had just pitched some hay to his horses when he heard a loud grunting SPANG and Velma's scream of anguish. The startled bog trotter, his bruised kisser high in the air, had run slam bang into the loaded clothes wire, stuck his toes into Velma's waiting clothesbasket, and turned an undignified wintersault up against a tree trunk.

The freezing washerwoman, hip deep in her private snow bank, turned loose a screechy yell of agony at the garment-and-wire-enshrouded villain who had now regained his feet. Velma's wails started the dazed bull into motion. Like most of his curious kind, he lumbered off in the direction he happened to be headed, which was around the cabin toward the barn. Ol' Bill, at a wheezing lope, was halfway up the shoveled path, when the bull, his horny umbrella festooned with laundry, snorted around the cabin with the clothes line and the frozen clothes trailing along behind him. He took one look at the puffing hillbilly, and mooselike, decided this was all Bill's fault. Old Snooty had a towel hanging on a lifter horn, and could only see out of one eye, but that was good enough. He lunged at Bill. He was brought up short by some of the clothes and wire snagging on the corner logs of the cabin.

This was only a slowed down interval. The irate washerwoman now

He reached his big smeller over.

had her second wind, and came up just in time to see the singing wire snag her best clothes on the log ends. Velma let out a frustrated scream whose velocity so jolted the big-nosed animal that he forgot poor Bill. He gave a worried squeal and trotted down the path. The wad of clothes sprung off the log ends at the impact of his weight. The wire whipped along behind with a gleeful hissing through the snow.

"Lookout, Bill, oh, that wire! Oh, Bill!" The jittery Bill was a little late. He jumped to one side, but it was the wrong one. The speeding lumps of clothes jerked him off his feet and trapped him in the kinky loops of wire. He was snaked along at a fast clip, with Velma screaming along in the rear, her speed slowed down by stray lumps of frozen clothing. The two work horses, hearing the hullaballoo and seeing the grunting apparition trotting towards them, ran frenzied around the corral in a race of their own. The flag waving moose burst into the open gate, the horses dashed past him and nearly ran over the snow-clouded procession behind. Old Big Nose gave a whining squeal when he came up to the high corral poles, but he didn't hesitate at a little thing like that, not with the following he had. He rared up in an ungainly leap and crashed over the corral. The clothesline, having suffered all the foolishness it could stand, kinked up and broke off in the noisy mess of splintered poles.

That bull moose was thrifty. He'd made a deposit on the manure pile and Bill was it. Velma couldn't stop now for hell or high water. She lit right on top of Bill, and he sank a foot deeper into his providential cushion.

The washerwoman jumped up to pull Bill out of his warm bed. When she saw that he was unhurt, she broke into tears of relief. The numbed victim tried to see where he was. What he heard was, "Well, this is *the absolute end*. I am going to renew my teacher's certificate, if we don't start wearing moosehide clothes!"

Bill sat up in bed, rubbed his face clear, and mumbled, "You thaid a mooseful!"

The Alcoholic

The ways of women and moose are strange, Bill thought as he hung out the re-washed clothes the next morning. "Here I am, an innocent bystander caught in the web. Innocent, hell, come to think it over, I shouldn'ta even seen the calf that spring, a-whinin' an' lookin' so needful of a friend. An' I thought *he* was innocent." Ol' Bill had one eye on the snowy timbered hillside above him, and the other towards the window where Velma was looking over the picture collection of her college days. The wind came up as Bill was hanging a heavy, fast freezing shirt on the sticky wire. An arm whipped up and the sleeve cuff whopped him square in his moose-watching eye. "By the Judas, even my own shirt's against me. Dang near got an eye out from that button. An' who'd think the skin'd come off, touchin' a bare wire with a wet hand. Why dang them clothespins. Bust up easy. Blame companies sure make things cheap nowadays. Thinkin' it over, I was sure lucky findin' all the clothes that blame moose drug around yesterday. Didn't seem ta hurt 'em much, either. Funny. Musta been th' heavy snow saved 'em—an' me—*and* Velma!"

Bill grinned to himself, thinking how angry Velma had been when she told about hiding under the pail. "Haw, woulda sure like t'of seen that, hidin' under a little pail. Thinkin' it over, though, she sure coulda been hurt bad from that moose. Damn him. Sure glad I only got a few more t'hang up, fingers a-freezin'. By George, I see now what a woman's got t'put up with, a-hangin' out clothes. Specially in winter." The wind had really got to blowing by now, and freezing clothes popped against each other. Bill blew on his fingers. His grin turned into a frustrated pucker as he worked on down the line. "Wouldncha know, everything come at once? First Moocher gets kicked an' his leg broke—hell, no, that was good luck, come t'think of it. If he hadn't been down t'town t'the vet's, mighta complicated this moose deal, seein' how he don't like moose. Well, then, the moose an' the manure pile—that was lucky, too, only Velma don't believe it. An' the radiator hoze on the buzz saw engine sprung a big leak 'n' I had t'saw wood by hand. Then last night Velma gets a toothache. Sure scared me, middle o' th'night. Wisdom tooth, she says. Better this mornin'. Then th'washin' machine engine breaks down. Velma

115

doesn't say a word, just hums college tunes 'n' plays them high-toned records on th'music box. Well, I sure was glad t'find that ol' scrubbin' board in th'bunkhouse. Washin' clothes by hand ain't no picnic, I'll tell a man. By damn, women do have it hard, when ya come t'think of it. I sure hope that hummin' 'n' talkin' about a teacher's certificate ain't serious. I wouldn't be able t'stand that."

On the porch, Bill rubbed his freezing fingers together and grabbed a broom to sweep the snow off his shoepacks. He was still talking to himself. "Damned if I'll ever have a pet moose again. By hell, she's still a-playin' them hi-flyin' records. I c'n see where she's scraped the frost off a window ta see if a moose scared me off. Why, damn th'things anyhow. No more pets for me—why, damn me fer a sap anyhow. That blame calf a-layin' there in th'willows that spring—innocent, hell, I was the innocent one. Sucker, hell, yes, sucker. That's me, might as well admit it. Dammit.

"Looks like we gotta go t'town now, an' th' snow too deep fer th' pickup. Dang th' early winter anyhow. Take Velma in t'git her tooth fixed—hope th'poor kid c'n stand th'snowshoe trip."

Bill stamped his way in the door, still mumbling, "Gotta fix up a list, le's see, yeah: Lower hose f'r buzz saw radiator. More anti-freeze alkyhaul—lost some before I got it drained. See Moocher at ol' Doc Frazier's—better not try t'bring him home, deep snow, cast on his leg. Spark plug 'n' condenser for washing machine. Damn moose anyhow. I know dern well this washday moose couldn'ta been Nosy. Naw, he wouldn't do a thing like that. Well, now, thinkin' it over—it just coulda been. A pet! A damned pet!"

Nosy the pet moose had gone back to his own kind two or three years ago, and since that time Bill had made no more pets out of lost mountain children. Bill found out he could get away with an occasional damn around the house, but moose was a bad word. He'd found that out the hard way.

Velma and Bill had a few visits from Nosy during the last two or three winters. The only way they could tell him from other moose was from the barbed wire cuts he'd suffered on his lower front legs. He would come in February or March after he'd shed his horns, so the scars were his only trademark. The dimly remembered handouts made him comically dangerous. But he stayed away after a few lumps were hammered on him in the hay corral. Velma swore Nosy was the laundry moose, but Bill wasn't sure. He hadn't really checked those front legs yesterday.

"If we can make it down to Murphy's ranch, we can get Johnny to

116

take us to town," Bill said as he was strapping Velma into her snow-shoes. "We ought to make the six miles easy enough. All downhill. Here, wrap that scarf up tight around your jaw." Velma doggedly plunked along in Bill's big tracks, bracing herself with a pole Bill gave here. The heavy snow on the old crust was hard traveling in, and she could barely see the wind-whipped trail ahead through the peephole above her scarf. That wisdom tooth in her swollen jaw ached from the knifing blasts.

Breaking trail about 40 feet ahead, Bill kept looking back anxiously at Velma. There were a few scattered moose feeding in the willow clumps along the river bottom below the road. They seemed to be minding their own business, so Bill gave them no more thought. The two travelers hit their stride and were making good time. Three miles to go, and the snow got thinner and easier to travel in.

Crunching along behind, intent on her painful problem, Velma suddenly had a new one. And wouldn't you know, it was moose. She heard a pleased grunt and a muffled yell. Stopped short, she saw a huge horned bull right in front of her. Bill was humped over sideways with one snowshoe waving in the air. The moose had his long snoot rammed in Bill's shoulder pack and was rooting around for a handout.

About that time, the grownup grafter found out never to fool around with a bad wisdom tooth. Bill was lucky again, even if Nosy did have one scarred foot punched through the rawhide filling of Bill's long-tailed web. Instincts had flared up from Velma's sea-faring ancestors, for Velma viciously harpooned the bull moose with her pole and then started hammering him on the stern. The bog trotter tried to match the mad woman's snarls, but when her pole broke across his suffering rump, he gave a choky whine and plunged off up the mountainside. He had a paper-wrapped lunch in his mouth and Bill's snowshoe above his knee. Every time he sank through the snow crust the web worked higher.

Velma had forgotten all about her tooth during the mixup with the grownup delinquent. Bill struggled up the hill above them and recovered the punctured web where Nosy had shed it. He found he could patch it up fair enough to hobble along on, and nothing else seemed to be damaged except frayed tempers.

About the time her wisdom tooth forgot the excitement and started throbbing again, Velma heard Bill give a big holler and saw him wave at a pickup away down on the snow-cleared county road far below them. It was Johnny Murphy and he was tooting the horn.

A few hours afterward Velma was safe at her sister Minnie's house

117

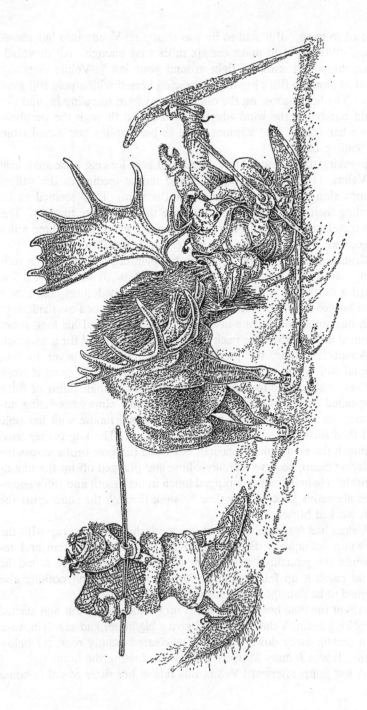

Velma harpooned the bull moose.

in town. Seemed the dentist was gone on a trip down to the county seat. Moocher was doing pretty good on three legs and a cast, and Minnie acted like she thought she could get along with him, too. But she didn't put out any objections when Bill said he had to get back to look after the milk cow and chickens, and run his line of marten and coyote traps. While Bill was filling up his knapsack in the store, John Murphy was busy loading his pickup with supplies for his own family.

"By George, you sure shoulda stuck your foot in my big mouth," Johnny Murphy looked at Bill with a grin. "That word *moose* must be a dirty one in your family." Johnny kidding about the lunch-stealing ruckus hadn't been funny to Velma. Now Bill added the story of the washday moose.

"Well, I reckon you're lucky at that, Bill. If that'd happened at my place I'd have had to wash all our clothes from now on. And we've got five kids."

"You know, Johnny, it's close to Christmas, and I've decided to give Velma a present she'll like. A resolution that I won't adopt any more pets."

Johnny, knowing Bill, says with a snicker, "Well, maybe not moose ones, anyhow. When things get dull down to my place, Bill, I'm going to come up and pay you a visit. You folks never seem to have a dull moment."

"By gosh, you do that, Johnny. We'll have everything except moose meat. I wouldn't eat that stuff on a bet."

Murphy hauled Bill and his plunder as far as he could, after he failed to persuade him to stay the night at his ranch. That was a couple of dark hours ago. The hillbilly was all worn out as he clunked up to his shadowy and snow-covered buildings. Last summer he had added a roof to connect his home cabin with the storehouse behind. Now the snow had drifted in on both sides. Ol' Bill unstrapped his snowshoes and stuck them tail down, upright in the snow. He fumbled with his pack straps and finally got his heavily loaded pack board off his weary shoulders.

After he slid down into the area-way to get his load into the storehouse, Bill thought he heard stealthy crunches in the rock-hard snow, banked eye level above him. He remembered willow crunching thieves and thought about the apples in his pack sack, but there were no more sounds out of the night. He leaned over to hang his pack on a nail until he could open the door, and stumbled and stuck a shoe pack into a washtub half full of the anti-freeze he had drained from his buzz saw engine.

119

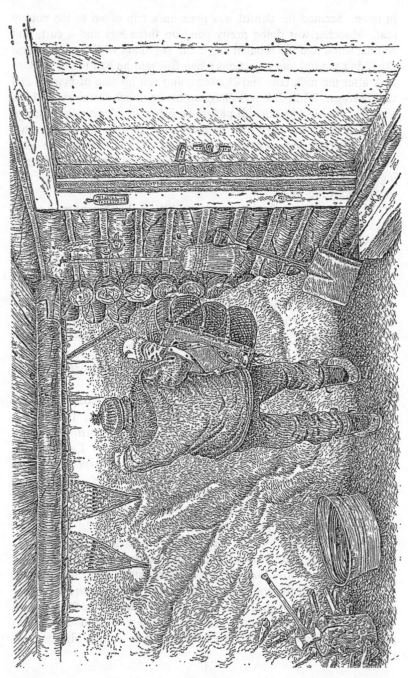

Bill thought he heard stealthy crunches.

Nosy couldn't stand it any more, he'd smelled apples for a mile, and here it was just about Christmas. So he took a chance and down he came. The soggy-footed rancher had just pried the frost-locked door open, when a thousand pounds of hairy Christmas resolution fell down against his weary carcass and shot him through the door right onto a pile of sacked oats. Ol' Bill was in but he was out.

The white-footed mouse had found it a tight squeeze through the knothole in the floor. She got her belly full, then she started back and forth, packing oats down under the floor boards. It looked like a long cold winter ahead, and sometimes hillbillies patch up knotholes. Mice, like men, know straight lines are the shortest, so Bill was brought to by strayed oats spilling down his open mouth. Strangled, he sat up and coughed out the grains. He lay back a minute listening to kicking thumps and unearthly groans. With a start he realized that he wasn't asleep at all. He fumbled under his heavy coat to the matches in his shirt pocket. He lit one and then limped over to the door, but the cold breeze flickered the small flame out. Just as Bill started to figure what had happened a thrashing hind foot of the trapped bog trotter caught him on his bruised hip and knocked him up against a cupboard. It crashed down on top of him. As he fell, he could hear Velma's new china set, as yet unused, get a breaking in that was going to be hard to explain.

It was dark again, but Bill's memory was afire and that kind of heat was uncomfortable in the frigid storehouse. Bill got up in a hurry, though, when he heard the gurgling and thumping sounds that finally died down to an uneasy silence. Reminded Bill of a drunken fight he'd seen once.

After that last gargling sigh in the area way, there wasn't a sound. Bill mustered up enough strength to stand up. He fumbled around in the dark and finally found another match. He remembered an old kerosene lantern hanging on a rafter nail above him. He got the lantern lit, and wobbled over to the open door to see the sights.

There was a huge bull moose lying belly side up with his head turned sharply to one side. He filled the whole space with his dark roan carcass. There were deep scars on the limp gray legs. It was Nosy come home to roost. Bill Thompson could see that the moose was defunct, and for once he was thankful. For that anyhow.

Nosy's magnificent set of horns had caught in a stack of split wood piled against the log wall, and his head was twisted at a grotesque angle, with his long snoot stuck into the washtub full of antifreeze.

121

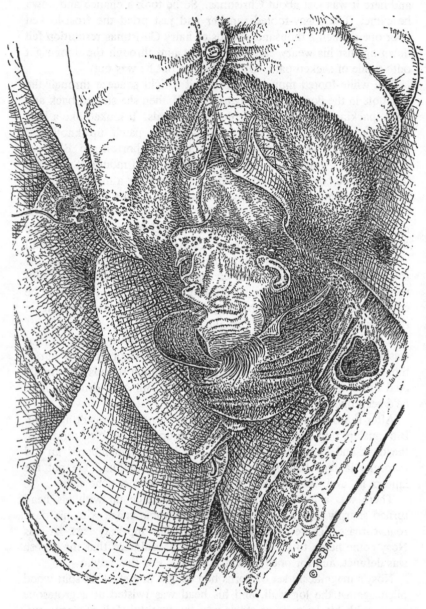

Bill was brought to by strayed oats.

Some apples from Bill's knocked-down pack floated around in the beverage.

Holding the flickering lantern high above him, Bill began to realize that Nosy really must have acquired bad habits out there in the wild blue yonder. The moose had died a drunk. Ol' Bill put his soaked shoepack up on the short-tailed burglar's limp carcass with a last farewell. He looked at his grownup pet and sadly said to himself: "Yessir, a plumb alcoholic. Too late now to join the alcoholic non-a-moose." Bill was a teetotaler himself.

Joe Back was born in Ohio in 1899 and moved to Wyoming when he was thirteen. He served as a machine gun instructor during World War I, then took up trade as a cowboy, guide, and packer. Later he spent four years at the Art Institute of Chicago where, to use Joe's words, he "damn near starved to death." Art education changed his life, however, and although he went back to packing and guiding, he also became nationally known as a sculptor. Joe Back died September 7, 1986 at age 87—through the magic of his illustrations and writing we celebrate and share his work.